The Outcasts of 19 Schuyler Place

Also by E. L. Konigsburg

e. l. konigsburg

The Outcasts of 19 Schuyler Place

ATHENEUM BOOKS FOR YOUNG READERS

New York   London   Toronto   Sydney

ATHENEUM BOOKS FOR YOUNG READERS
An imprint of Simon & Schuster Children's Publishing Division
1230 Avenue of the Americas
New York, New York 10020

Book design by O'Lanso Gabbidon

The text for this book is set in Bembo.
Printed in the United States of America
First Edition

10 9 8 7 6 5 4 3 2 1

Library of Congress Cataloging-in-Publication Data
Konigsburg, E. L.
The outcasts of 19 Schuyler Place / E. L. Konigsburg.—1st ed.
p.   cm.
Summary: Upon leaving an oppressive summer camp, twelve-year-old Margaret Rose Kane spearheads a campaign to preserve three unique towers her great-uncles have been building in their backyard for more than forty years.
ISBN 0-689-86636-4
[1. Social action—Fiction. 2. Individuality—Fiction. 3. Uncles—Fiction. 4. Hungarian Americans—Fiction. 5. Camp—Fiction.]
I. Title: Outcasts of nineteen Schuyler Place. II. Title.
PZ7 .K8352Ou   2004
[Fic]—dc21   2003008067

This book is for David and for Jean,
who cheered its conception but sadly left it an orphan
before birth.

The Outcasts of 19 Schuyler Place

The year that I was twelve:

Sally Ride became the first American woman in space
and
El Niño, a warming of the ocean water off the coast of Peru, affected weather worldwide and caused disasters on almost every continent on planet Earth. At El Niño's peak the day was 0.2 milliseconds longer because the angle of Earth shifted
and
President Ronald Reagan signed legislation declaring that Martin Luther King Jr. had been born on the third Monday of every January, and henceforth the day(s) of his birth would be a legal holiday in our nation
and
AT&T, the giant telephone company called Ma Bell, broke up and gave birth to several independent low-cost long-distance communications companies
and
The Federal Communications Commission authorized Motorola to begin testing cellular phone services in Chicago

and

*Cabbage Patch dolls were selling so fast, merchants couldn't
keep them on the shelves.*

All of that is history now. And, fortunately, so is the
story I am about to tell. It begins when Uncle Alex
retrieved me from summer camp.

Bartleby at Talequa

one

Uncle Alex was sweating when he arrived at Camp Talequa. No wonder. The Greyhound bus had left him off at the point where the camp road meets the highway, and it was all uphill from there. The camp road was not paved but laid with rough gravel. It was July, and it had not rained for three weeks. Uncle walked those three dusty miles wearing wing-tip, leather-soled oxfords; a long-sleeved, buttoned-up shirt; suit jacket; necktie; and a Borsalino hat. Tartufo, his dog, walked at his side. He had bought his hat, his shoes, and his dog in Italy. His hat was tan, his shoes brown, and his dog was white with brown spots, but by the time they arrived at the office, all were gray with gravel dust.

Not until he was standing in front of the camp office did Uncle remove his Borsalino or put a leash on Tartufo. He stood on the bottom of the three steps leading to the office door and flicked the dust from his hat and, as much as he could, from Tartufo's paws. With his handkerchief, he wiped first his forehead and then his shoes. Having a shine on his shoes was an Old World point of pride.

Holding his hat against his chest and Tartufo's leash with one hand, he knocked on the office door with the other.

Mrs. Kaplan, the camp director, called, "Who is it?" and Uncle stepped inside. He told her that he was Alexander Rose and that he had come to take Margaret home.

For the best part of a minute, Mrs. Kaplan was speechless. At last she said, "And just *who* are you?"

"I am Margaret's uncle, Alexander Rose. Don't you remember? We spoke on the phone last night."

Mrs. Kaplan had called shortly before nine. After introducing herself she had said, "We are calling, Mr. Rose, because Margaret seems to be having a bit of a problem adjusting to camp life."

"What have you done?" he had asked.

"Everything," she replied. "We have done everything we know how to do, but she is totally unresponsive. When we ask her to do something—anything—she says, 'I prefer not to.'"

"Let me talk to her."

"We can't do that, Mr. Rose. Campers are to have no contact with their caregivers until the two-week adjustment period is over. We cannot make exceptions."

"Then how can I possibly help?"

"We would like your input on how we can help her *want* to participate. We do not like to force our campers to participate."

"I suggest you change your activities."

"We can't do that, Mr. Rose. We cannot tailor our activities to every single child in this camp. As a matter of fact, it is the very nature of the activities we offer that sets Talequa apart from all the other camps. We want Margaret to fit in, Mr. Rose."

"Let me think about this," he said. "I'll be in touch."

Uncle had thought about it and decided that the best thing he could do would be to go directly to Camp Talequa and bring me back with him.

Staying with my uncles—Alex, who was an old bachelor, and Morris, his brother, a widower—had been one of my two first choices of "What to do with Margaret" while my parents were in Peru. The Uncles lived in an old house on Schuyler Place. I loved them, their house, and their garden.

—them

I loved their Old World habits. Like wearing a Borsalino hat from Italy instead of a baseball cap. Neither one of them owned a baseball cap. Or blue jeans. Or sneakers. Or a sports shirt. They never watched sports on TV and had never been to a football game, even when the home team, Clarion State University, was playing. They could speak three languages besides English. They had wine with dinner every night and ate so late that sometimes it was midnight when they finished. They served coffee with real cream and lump sugar that they dropped into the cup with a tiny pair of tongs. They had never eaten at a McDonald's or standing up. Even in the summer when they ate in their garden, they still covered their table with a white linen cloth, served their wine in crystal goblets, and their food on china dishes. And they never hurried through dinner. If it got to be too late when they finished eating, they would leave unwashed dishes in the sink and go to bed.

—their house

I loved 19 Schuyler Place. It was within walking distance of Town Square, a city bus stop, the main library, and the pedestrian mall downtown. I loved sleeping over. Two years before, when I was only ten, they had allowed me to pick out the furniture for the bedroom that they told me would be mine whenever I came to visit. They took me to Sears in the Fivemile Creek Mall and let me choose. I chose a bedroom *suite* with only one twin bed (the room was small) in genuine French provincial style, white with gold-tone accents. When it was delivered, Uncle Morris had said, "Very distinguished," and Uncle Alex proclaimed it, "Quite elegant." I was so convinced that they approved of everything I did that I believed them.

—their garden

Their garden was unlike any other in the neighborhood—or the world. Like all the others nearby, theirs had started out as a long, narrow yard that stretched from the service porch in back of the house to the alley, but the resemblance stopped where it started.

The Uncles had unevenly divided their backyard space lengthwise into two thirds and one third. They further divided the narrower, one-third section, in half, crosswise. In the narrow third closest to the house, Uncle Morris raised peppers. They grew in shapes from bell to cornucopia and in flavors from sweet to jalapeño. Their colors were red, yellow, purple, and every shade of green from lime to pine. The other half of the narrow third was planted with roses. Entirely with roses. Some were trained to grow along the iron pipe fence that separated their yard from their neighbor's at number 17. Others grew in their own hoed crater of earth. Some blossoms were quiet and tiny as a bud; others were loud and six inches wide. There were

many varieties, many sizes, but they were a symphony
of a single chord, for all of them were rose colored—
blooming in every shade from delicate to brazen, from
blush to Pepto-Bismol.

In the larger section, the two-thirds, wider strip, were
the towers. There were three of them. They zigged and
zagged along the perimeter of the fence that separated
my uncles' yard from their neighbor's at number 21.
They soared over the rooftop of their house and every
other house in the neighborhood. The tallest was Tower
Two, so called because it was the second one built, and
it was closest to the house. Tower Three was in the slant
middle.

My uncles had been building them for the past
forty-five years.

Even though all of the towers were taller than any of
the two-story houses in the neighborhood, even though
they were made of steel, they did not darken the space
around them. They were built of a network of ribs and
struts that cast more light than shadow. Like a spider-
web, they were strong but delicate. From each of the
rungs, from each section of each of the rungs, dangled
thousands—*thousands*—of chips of glass and shards of
porcelain and the inner workings of old clocks. Some
of the pendants were short and hugged the horizontal
ribs, while others dangled on long threads of copper. In

some places, a single wire held two drops of glass, one under the other; in other places, there were three—dangling consecutively, one beneath the other. Some of the pendants were evenly spaced in groups of three or four. Some were bunched together like the sixteenth notes on a musical staff followed by a single large porcelain bob—a whole note rest. On another rung, or perhaps at a distance on the same rung, a series of evenly spaced glass drops dangled in a rainbow of colors.

Like gypsy music (my uncles were Hungarian), the pendants hung in a rhythm that is learned but cannot be taught.

The towers were painted. Not solemnly but astonishingly. Astoundingly. There were carnival shades of mauve and violet, ochre and rose, bright pink and orange sherbet, and all the colors were stop-and-go, mottled into a camouflage pattern. Lavender pink met lime green in the middle of a rung, or cerulean blue climbed only halfway up a vertical axis until it met aquamarine.

On top of the tallest tower, fixed in place, were four clock faces, none of which were alike. Atop the other two towers was a single clock face on a swivel that rotated with the wind. The clock faces had no hands.

I loved standing under the towers—choose any one, depending on the time of day—looking up and farther up, until the back of my head rested on my shoulders. I would hang there until a certain slant of light caught the pendants and made them refract an endless pattern of colors. And then, and then I would spin around and around, making myself the moving sleeve of a kaleidoscope. And when I stopped, I would look down and watch their still-spinning shadow embroider the ground.

I had always loved spending time at 19 Schuyler Place, and I thought that my uncles loved having me. I expected them to jump at a chance to have me spend the four summer weeks that my parents would be gone. But they had not.

My other first choice of "What to do with Margaret" had been to go with my parents to Peru. They had always taken me with them before. I had assumed they would want me along because as an only child, I had spent a great deal of time among adults, and I was an excellent traveling companion. I never required extra bathroom stops—my mother always carried empty cottage cheese containers as an emergency portable potty—never demanded special foods, and regardless of how endless the car ride was, I never asked, "Are we there yet?"

Since I was not given either of my two first choices, the only remaining alternative was summer camp. That being the case, I decided that the choice of camp would be mine and mine alone. So it was with a bruised heart and wounded pride that I set about making my selection. I decided that I would choose such a wonderful camp and have such a wonderful time that my parents and my uncles would be sorry that they had not come, too.

I invested many hours in making my decision. I sent away for thirty-six brochures, read them all, and sent away for thirty-two tapes, of which I watched a total of nineteen all the way through. I chose Talequa.

After recovering from the shock of Uncle's unannounced appearance, Mrs. Kaplan asked, "Why, Mr. Rose, did you not give us notice of your arrival?"

"Because if I had, Mrs. Kaplan," he replied, "you would have told me not to come."

That was true, but she did not have to admit or deny it. "How did you get here?" she asked.

"I walked."

No one walked into Camp Talequa. Visitors arrived by car or minivan and by invitation. Mrs. Kaplan had heard that once, long before she had bought the camp, an elderly couple had arrived in a taxi, but there were no living witnesses to that story, so she placed it into the category of creation myth. But even if there really had once been a couple who had arrived in a taxi, no one had ever *walked* into Camp Talequa. There was no rule against it because who would have dreamed that such a rule would be necessary? Actually, there were no rules at all about *how* to arrive, but the Talequa handbook made it clear that there were definite rules about *when.* One strict rule was: No visits from friends or relatives for the first two weeks of a session, which, in Mrs. Kaplan's interpretation, made Alexander Rose a trespasser. There were other rules—rules about what you could bring with you. Alcohol and drugs were explicitly forbidden, of course, but it was just as clearly written, so were dogs. The punishment for bringing a dog was not as well defined as that for alcohol or drugs (immediate, nonrefundable expulsion), but the basic animal rule was: Dogs were not allowed in camp. Never. Paper trained, potty trained, K-9 trained: No. Even if they were trained to flush, they were not allowed. There was to be no Lassie, no Pluto, no Scooby-Doo. Never. Not as visitors. Not *with* visitors.

And this man had brought a dog!

Collecting her wits, Mrs. Kaplan presented Uncle with her best varnished smile. "We are most willing to discuss Margaret's problem with you," she declared, "but, Mr. Rose, we cannot permit dogs on our premises."

Alexander Rose knew that any smile that registered

as high on the gloss meter as Mrs. Kaplan's came from well-practiced insincerity. Uncle also knew that Mrs. Kaplan did not object to Tartufo as much as she objected to his disobeying one—no, really *two*—of her rules. He could have told her that Tartufo was a working dog and allowed to go where no dog had gone before. He could have asked her, Would an ordinary dog be allowed on a Greyhound? But, wisely, he didn't tell, and he didn't ask. Instead, he said, "Tartufo is here, Mrs. Kaplan. I'm not a magician. I cannot make him disappear."

With her smile lashed to her teeth, Mrs. Kaplan replied, "Then we must insist that it wait outside."

Uncle had learned long ago that obeying a rule in fact but not in spirit was very hard on people who say *we* for *I* and who do not allow dogs on their premises. So without hesitation, he led Tartufo to a spot just outside the front door of the office cabin. With the door open so that Mrs. Kaplan could hear, he told Tartufo to sit. Then he removed Tartufo's leash and carried it back into the office.

When he reentered, Mrs. Kaplan had her back to him. She was removing a file folder from a cabinet behind her desk. Uncle stood in front of the desk, conspicuously holding the empty leash in his hand. When she turned around and saw the leash, she realized that not only was there a dog on her premises, but it was not tethered. The smile left her face, and her mouth formed a Gothic O. She started to say something, thought better of it, and didn't. Instead, she sat down, opened the file, and began studying it. The file was all about me, Margaret Rose. Considering that this was only my ninth day at camp, the folder was quite full.

Uncle continued to stand, waiting for Mrs. Kaplan to look up again. "May I be seated?" he asked.

"Please," she said, sweeping her hand toward the right chair, one of two that faced her desk.

Uncle sat down, quickly got up and moved the chair four inches, sat down, got up and moved it again in the opposite direction, and then did it a third time. "What seems to be the problem, Mr. Rose?"

"The sun," he said. "It's shining in my eyes, and you are a dark shadow." Uncle meant every word.

Wearing her patience like a body stocking, Mrs. Kaplan said, "Suppose you take the other chair."

"Good idea," Uncle said, and moved that chair once before settling down. With a fussiness as elaborate as it was deliberate, he inched his bottom toward the back of the chair. He steadied his gaze on the woman sitting across the desk from him and waited until only the sheerest shroud of patience remained. Then he folded his hands in his lap and said, "Now we can talk."

In more ways than one, Alexander Rose resembled a set of Matryoshka nesting dolls. He was short and squat, he had many fully formed layers beneath his roly-poly outer shell, and deep inside was an innermost self, a core that was solid and indivisible.

In an unconscious effort to create as much distance as possible between them, Mrs. Kaplan leaned back in her chair and slowly turned the full force of an uppish smile on him. "We see, Mr. Rose, that you are not this child's parent."

"That is correct. I am her granduncle."

"You must mean *great*-uncle."

"Great or grand, they mean the same: I am the brother of her grandmother." Mrs. Kaplan was not sure if *great-uncle* and *granduncle* were interchangeable, but she decided to let his remark go. She would check it later. Uncle said, "At the moment, though, since Margaret's parents are out of the country and unable to tend to her, I am *in loco parentis*, in the position of a parent."

Mrs. Kaplan replied, "We know perfectly well what *in loco parentis* means, Mr. Rose." But as soon as she said it, she regretted it. This interview was not going well. Best to get to the matter at hand. "Yes, it was in your capacity as guardian of Margaret that I called you last night. As I mentioned on the phone, Margaret refuses to participate in any of our activities. She says, 'I prefer not to.'" Tapping the folder, she said, "We have here a report from Gloria, Margaret's camp counselor." She lowered her head, put on her glasses, and began reading aloud. "On Monday—

> Margaret did not take a copy of the words to our camp songs when I was passing them out. I did not force a copy on her because I assumed that like a lot of our other girls, she had learned the words from our tape. Then on Tuesday, our karaoke and sing-along evening, she did not sing with the group. When I asked her why, she said it was because she didn't know the words."

Mrs. Kaplan raised her voice slightly while reading the phrase *because she didn't know the words.* She looked over her reading glasses at Uncle and waited until he indicated with a nod that he had caught the significance of her emphasis. She continued, "On Wednesday—

> Margaret did not show up for origami class. When I went to her cabin to fetch her, she refused to attend. When I asked her why, she said that she preferred not to.

Margaret failed to create a design to paint on a T-shirt. She said that she preferred not to. Then in the afternoon when we were to paint the T-shirts, she said she couldn't because she didn't have a design. I suggested that she do something spontaneous—an abstract, maybe—and she replied, 'I prefer not to.'"

Uncle folded his hands across the expanse of his belly and cocked his head a little to the left, his supreme listening mode. He waited.

Mrs. Kaplan took off her reading glasses and laid them on top of the open folder. "That brings us to the events of yesterday. The girls were scheduled to go tubing on the lake. Everyone but Margaret boarded the bus. Everyone waited, and when Margaret did not appear, Gloria went to Meadowlark cabin to look for her. She found Margaret still in her bunk, not ready. We had to leave without her. A little later, we personally went to her cabin to have a talk with her."

Mrs. Kaplan waited for a response from Uncle. None came. She cleared her throat and continued. "Our visit yesterday elicited a remark from your niece, Mr. Rose, that was so uncalled for that we were prompted to phone you last evening." She again waited for a response from Uncle, expecting him to ask what awful thing I had said, but Uncle asked nothing. In truth, he did not want to possibly have to agree with Mrs. Kaplan that something I had said was truly uncalled for. When it became clear that Uncle would not ask, she continued. "Your niece has become increasingly unreachable." She put her glasses back on, took two pages from the folder, and handed them to Uncle. "You will find that Louise Starr, our camp nurse, agrees. You may read her reports."

She handed Uncle Alex the forms. The first report said that I, Margaret Rose Kane, was neither anorexic nor bulimic nor suffering from preadolescent depression. *In conclusion, I find her simply uncooperative.* The second report again eliminated the same things—bulimia, anorexia, and depression—and upgraded me from *uncooperative* to *incorrigible.*

Uncle Alex was not a rapid reader, and he took the time to read the reports twice before laying the sheets back down on the desk. He slowly pushed them toward Mrs. Kaplan. He said nothing. Mrs. Kaplan closed the folder, removed her glasses, and rested her hands on the cover. "What do you have to say about those reports, Mr. Rose?"

"Nurse Starr has a very nice handwriting," he replied.

"Is that all you have to say?"

"Yes, it is all I have to say. Not all I *can* say."

"Please feel free to tell us what is on your mind."

"Well, Mrs. Kaplan, I can tell you that I understand. You see, I, too, once lived under a monarchy. I, too, preferred not to, so I emigrated."

"We would hardly call our community here at Camp Talequa a monarchy, Mr. Rose."

"And that, Mrs. Kaplan, is because you are the queen."

"We deeply resent that remark, Mr. Rose."

"I'm sure you do, Mrs. Kaplan, but with all due respect, your camp here has a surprising resemblance to the camps in my old country. You require blind obedience. So did they. You demand conformity. So did they." Uncle then waved a hand toward the folder. "You have your spies. They had theirs. And you have—"

"We have happy campers, Mr. Rose."

"And so you should, Mrs. Kaplan. And it is for that very reason that I want to remove an unhappy one." He stood up. "Now, if you'll please tell me where I can find Margaret Rose, I will get her, and we shall leave."

Mrs. Kaplan protested. "We have procedures, Mr. Rose."

"Start the procedures."

"There are forms to be signed."

"Bring them to me. I will sign them."

Mrs. Kaplan resisted. Uncle insisted. Finally, Mrs.
Kaplan called over to the main house and asked Gloria
to come to the office. As they waited, Uncle asked Mrs.
Kaplan for a refund.

"A refund, Mr. Rose?"

"Yes, Mrs. Kaplan. It is my understanding that all the
fees were paid in advance. I expect you to deduct from
my refund the eight and a half days Margaret Rose has
spent here plus something for your administrative costs."

"But surely, Mr. Rose, you know that we are at a
total loss."

"Surely you have a waiting list. Most places do."

"Of course we have a waiting list. *Certainly* we have
a waiting list. We have a long waiting list. Our waiting
list is as long as that of any camp in the Adirondacks.
But at this late date, there is no way we can sell the
space that was to have been taken by Margaret. Our
supplies have been ordered with a certain number in
mind. That number includes Margaret Kane." She
pulled a sheet from a file drawer and thrust it at Uncle
Alex. "Read your contract. No refunds after June
twenty-first. There will be no refund, Mr. Rose."

"That being the case, Mrs. Kaplan, I would appreci-
ate some lunch and a ride back to Epiphany."

"We can allow lunch, Mr. Rose. But a ride back to
Epiphany is out of the question. We cannot tie up a bus

and a driver to transport two people all the way to Epiphany."

"Not a bus, Mrs. Kaplan. A van."

"We have no van, Mr. Rose."

"Do we have a car, Mrs. Kaplan?"

Mrs. Kaplan gritted her teeth. "Yes, we have a car, Mr. Rose."

"That will do nicely," he replied.

Mrs. Kaplan pushed a sheath of papers across the desk and handed Uncle a pen. "We are a business, Mr. Rose. A ride back to Epiphany is all we can afford. Time is money, Mr. Rose."

"Time is not money, Mrs. Kaplan. Time wasted is often time well spent. Money wasted is merely redistributed." Uncle signed the papers with a flourish and then took a plastic bag from his jacket pocket. From the bag, he took a rag and said to Mrs. Kaplan, "If Margaret Rose comes while I'm gone, please tell her that I'm burying the rag. She'll understand what it is that I am doing."

"And just what is it that you will be doing?" Mrs. Kaplan demanded. Uncle explained that he was training Tartufo to be a truffle dog. "Tartufo means truffle in Italian, Mrs. Kaplan. The rag is soaked in truffle oil. I will bury the rag out in your woods and have Tartufo retrieve it."

"We do not allow dogs on our premises, and we have no chocolate in camp. Certainly no buried chocolate."

"The truffles of which I speak are underground mushrooms, Mrs. Kaplan. A natural food."

"Whatever," Mrs. Kaplan said. "But of this I am certain: There will be no dog loose in our woods. I repeat: No dogs in our woods."

"Whatever," Uncle said with a smile, replacing the truffle rag back in the bag.

That is when Gloria came into the office. Mrs. Kaplan told her to help Margaret Kane collect her belongings and bring them to the office. She did not introduce Uncle, but as Gloria turned to carry out her orders, Uncle introduced himself. "May I ask," he said, "what kind of sandwiches you had for lunch today?" Gloria told him there had been tuna and bologna. With a childlike delight, he exclaimed, "That's what I guessed. To myself, I guessed sandwiches, and I guessed tuna and bologna." To Gloria, he said, "We'll take two tuna each. That'll be a total of four. With lettuce. We prefer whole wheat bread. Toasted."

Turning to Mrs. Kaplan, he said, "Toasting helps to keep the bread from getting soggy." Again addressing Gloria, he said, "I'll bet you had chocolate chip"—he glanced mischievously at Mrs. Kaplan and corrected himself—"*some* kind of chip cookies for dessert, and I'll bet you have a couple of those left, too." Gloria looked toward Mrs. Kaplan for a quick check before nodding. "And milk?" he asked. Gloria nodded again. "We'll have two containers of milk, please."

Mrs. Kaplan picked up the phone. "We'll call the kitchen with your order to save time."

Uncle waited until Gloria left, and then, holding the plastic bag in one hand and the disconnected leash in the other, he spun around, examining the four walls of fake paneling. "Yes," he said, half to himself, "tuna and bologna."

Uncle shrugged and smiled at Mrs. Kaplan. And she knew that Mr. Alexander Rose had gotten everything he had come for: the sandwiches, the ride back, and, most of all, *me*.

two

Jake the handyman was assigned to drive us back to Epiphany. I recognized him because he had been called to Meadowlark cabin three times. The first time was to exchange a bunk mattress—mine. The second time was to make a shower that wouldn't drain, drain, and the third time was to clean up a mess. Each time he came, he shuffled in, fixed what he was supposed to, and left without saying a word. He seemed borderline autistic, which would be Asperger's disorder, or mentally retarded, which would be fragile X syndrome. Both disorders are known to occur more frequently in males than in females. Because of his mental problem—whatever it was—I wasn't certain that he recognized me. I also wasn't certain that he should be driving a car. Uncle didn't seem worried. Of course, Uncle was hardly one to judge. His lack of driving skills was in the court records.

We were being driven through the Adirondacks, which according to the brochure is *"the beautiful setting of Camp Talequa, where campers have at their disposal the pristine riches of Mother Nature plus the convenience of our camp facilities, the warm companionship of fellow campers, and the friendly guidance of experienced counselors."*

—the pristine riches of Mother Nature
On the first evening, after everyone's parents had departed, we were sprayed with insect repellent and invited into Talequa's pristine riches to hear Mrs. Kaplan give her *Welcome, Campers* talk.

—the convenience of our camp facilities
The camp was divided into eight cabins. Eight girls in each cabin. Each cabin had a bird name. Each cabin door had a picture of its bird. There was: Hummingbird (the youngest, all eight-year-olds), Nightingale, Bobwhite, Cardinal, Oriole, Robin, Blue Jay, and Meadowlark. I was to be a Meadowlark. We were all twelve years old.

Being an only child, I had always had a room of my own, so I went off to my assigned cabin curious about what it would be like to share night-breathing with seven other girls.

That first night, our cabin counselor, Gloria Goldsmith—we were to call her Gloria—put slips of paper numbered 1 to 8 into a bowl and told us to pick one. The number on our paper would be the order in which we would choose our beds. All the cabins were alike: two bunk beds along each of the long walls, one bed on either side of the window. The bathroom—two shower stalls, two toilet stalls, and four sinks—was against the short wall in the back, opposite the door.

By a small margin, the best bed was the top bunk by the window farthest from the door. The worst, the bottom bunk closest to the door. But there was not much difference among them.

Of the eight Meadowlarks, I was the only one who had never been to a sleep-away camp before, and Berkeley Sims was the only one who had not been to Talequa before, although she had been to one camp or another every summer since she was nine years old. The other six all knew each other. This would be their third year at camp, their third at Talequa. They knew the songs, the schedule, the counselors—everything. They were the Alums. There were other alums scattered throughout the camp, but the Meadowlark Alums had made rooming together a condition of their coming to Talequa.

Alum Ashley Schwartz got #1 and picked the top bunk away from the door. I got #2 and picked the other top bunk away from the door. The third top bunk went to Alum Blair Patayani, and Berkeley Sims, the other new girl, got #4. She picked the remaining top bunk.

Gloria assigned us a cubby nearest our bunk and

reminded us that there were to be no showers after ten and that lights-out would be at ten thirty. Beds were to be made every morning before we left the cabin. "Any questions?" she asked. There were none, so she left to do some paperwork.

Gloria was hardly out the door before Alum Ashley Schwartz asked Berkeley Sims and me to switch beds with Heather Featherstone and Alicia Silver. Alicia had drawn a lower bunk by the door, and Heather had drawn the lower under mine. Berkeley agreed to switch and immediately started climbing down from the upper bunk. Ashley then said to me, "Heather will help you move your things."

And I replied, "That won't be necessary."

Surprised, Ashley asked, "Why?"

"Because I'm not switching."

Heather asked, "Why?"

And I said, "Because I prefer not to." That was the first time I said it.

—the warm companionship of fellow campers

The morning after bed selection, I went to breakfast with the seven other Meadowlarks. Berkeley Sims and I sat next to each other on one side of the table, and the Alums crowded together across from us. They seemed curious about Berkeley and me.

Berkeley was also an only child. Her mother and father were divorced, and her father sent her to camp every summer to use up most of his custody time. She had been to tennis camp when she was nine, to water-skiing camp when she was ten, and to cheerleading camp last year. Alicia Silver said, "You'll like Talequa better. It's not just one thing. It's crafts and nature study and some sports, like swimming." The other girls nodded in agreement. In one version or another, they all said the same thing: that Camp Talequa offered variety.

Berkeley's history made mine seem boring. I told them that my parents were still married—that summer they still were—and that my mother was a professor in the Psychology Department at Clarion State University and that my father was the registrar. Blair Patayani said that Clarion State was where her mother and father had gone to college and where they had met. The girls all seemed friendly enough.

I was curious about Berkeley, the other new girl. Having grown up with two parents who worked at a university, I knew that Berkeley in California was the home of a campus of the University of California, famous for sit-ins and very liberal political views. My father did not approve of sit-ins or liberal political views. My father did not approve of California, except for the fact that it had given us Ronald Reagan, who was the president of the United States at the time. My father loved President Reagan.

"Is Berkeley where you were born?" I asked.

"Where I was conceived," she answered.

Which stopped conversation until Heather Featherstone (whose name was also a little strange) smiled slyly and explained that while we were in camp, real names did not matter because the Alums called each other by their nicknames.

"What shall I call you?" I asked.

"I can't tell you," Heather replied. "Our nicknames are secret. We can't tell you until you have one of your own."

"I don't have a nickname," I replied. "Everyone calls me Margaret or Margaret Rose. Rose is my middle name."

Heather looked to her left at Ashley Schwartz and to her right at Kaitlin Lorenzo before saying, "Well, you don't give yourself a nickname. We give you one." The three of them nodded.

"How can you do that?" I asked. "A name is something your parents give you—just like your parents gave you Heather."

Ashley Schwartz joined in. "We're talking about a nickname—not something you put on a report card. After we give you a nickname, we tell you ours."

Kaitlin said, "Everyone has to have a nickname."

And I thought to myself: I don't.

After breakfast, we were divided into three groups in a mix-and-match arrangement of ages and cabins. We were to do a round-robin of lessons from each of three instructors who had gone to clown school. I was separated from the other Meadowlarks.

When I returned to the cabin during the break between makeup and juggling, I found that my bedclothes were all rumpled even though I had made my bed before leaving. I climbed up to my bunk. My covers had been pulled back, and a big wet spot filled the center of the mattress. I smelled urine.

Furious, I climbed down and waited for the other Meadowlarks to appear. I was determined to find out who had done this and confront her. I waited, and no one came. I didn't know where they were or what they were doing, but I knew that wherever and whatever, they were together, and it had all been worked out beforehand.

—and the friendly guidance of experienced counselors
I set out to look for my counselor and found her in the mess hall talking to the other counselors. I approached and asked if I could have a word with her in private. Gloria looked concerned as we walked to a far corner of the room where no one could hear us. I described what I had found in the cabin.

Gloria put a hand on my shoulder and said, "It's all right, Margaret. A lot of girls have accidents. After all, it's a strange bed. These are unfamiliar surroundings."

I protested, "But *I* didn't wet my bed. Someone else did."

"Sure. Sure. I understand." Gloria all but winked when she said that she would let the wet bed be a secret between us. "I'll just tell Jake to take the old mattress away and bring in a new one."

"But I didn't do it."

"We know, we know," Gloria replied. "Don't worry about it. It will be taken care of."

I persisted. "You saw that my bed was made this morning before I left the cabin. Didn't you?"

Gloria replied, "That's probably why the spot didn't dry out."

"My bed was not wet when I made it this morning. I did not wet it. Someone else did."

Gloria said, "That will be awful hard to prove."

I realized that, yes, it would be. The evidence was stacked against me. I started to walk away.

Gloria called me back. Bending close to my ear so that no one else could hear, she said, "I'll have Jake change the mattress before lunch. We'll not say anything to anyone about this. I won't even do the paperwork on it."

—warm companionship

The Alums were not as subtle as they thought they were. At dinner Ashley said that she had requested a room deodorant because she had detected a strange odor when she came into the cabin after clown class. Then, after a sliding glance at me, Kaitlin volunteered that her mother had sent her an extra set of sheets in case anyone in Meadowlark needed them. Alicia said that she had a friend whose little brother was a habitual bed wetter, and he had a rubber sheet on his bed "for precautionary reasons." Stacey said, "I hope no one in Meadowlark has to. I heard that they make your bed real hot."

In the evening the Alums whispered their secret nicknames to each other. By careful listening, I learned that Stacey Mouganis was named *Dolly* because she had one of the expensive handmade, not manufactured, Cabbage Patch dolls that she had brought with her to camp and, apparently, everywhere else. Heather Featherstone was *Fringie* because that was what she called the worn, cotton security blanket she could not sleep without. Ashley Schwartz was *Tattoo* because she had one. She was proud of her tattoo and often let it show while she was getting dressed or undressed. I heard her tell Berkeley that her parents had never seen it. I couldn't decide if she was bragging about how modest she was or how little her parents saw of her. Kaitlin Lorenzo was *B-Cup*, because that was her size, of which she was very proud. And even though I, too, would have been proud to be a B-cup, I would never call them by name. I would just let them B.

By the evening of the second day, they had given Berkeley her nickname. I had had no trouble finding out what it was. They had chosen *Metalmouth* for her. She wore braces. Although I could tell that the Alums were proud of their choice, I thought it was unimaginative. I knew they wanted me to hear so that I wouldn't want to be the only one left out of their secret nickname society.

On the evening of the third day, Ashley Schwartz approached. She asked me to please step down from my bunk so that they could initiate me. The Meadowlarks had thought of a wonderful nickname for me.

I didn't want one.

I liked my real name.

Names were important. Uncle Alex had told me about how language was God's gift to man, how God had asked Adam to name the animals, so He brought every beast of the field and every fowl of the air to Adam and let Adam name them. Naming was so important that it was the second thing God asked Adam to do.

I was Margaret. Margaret Rose. Margaret Rose

Kane. I had been named for my mother's mother, Margaret Rose Landau, who had died the summer before I was born. Rose had been her maiden name; she was the Uncles' sister. Uncle Morris had once told me, "Rose is your middle name, and don't you forget it. That Rose in the middle holds *Margaret* and *Kane* together, and it will stop bullets if you let it."

So far it had taken me twelve years to become Margaret Rose, and in the company of the Meadowlarks, I was finding it harder and harder to be her—or the Margaret Rose I thought I was.

Without coming down from my bunk, I said to the girls who had gathered around that I would like to know what name they had chosen for me.

"Come on down and find out," Alicia said.

Blair Patayani said that they couldn't possibly reveal my name in advance.

"Then I can't accept it," I said.

Heather thought I was teasing and said, "Aw, c'mon down."

I simply could not allow seven girls who hardly knew me to boil me down to a single word of their choosing.

Beckoning with her fingers, Ashley said, "Come on down now."

And I said, "I prefer not to."

That evening, by unanimous vote—Metalmouth's included—the Meadowlarks changed their choice of nicknames for me. I never found out what their first choice had been, for the one they whispered and that I was definitely meant to hear was *Diapers*. It was supposed to humiliate me, but instead it made me understand what Uncle Morris had meant about my real name stopping bullets.

three

The highway had broadened to six lanes when Tartufo nudged his face forward onto the seat cushion and whimpered an invitation to be petted. "Tartufo," I said. I waited for him to look at me and tilt his head, his sweet gesture that showed that he was ready to listen. "Tartufo," I repeated. "Do you like your name?" I held his face in my hands and brought my face close to his. "It's a good name, isn't it. I like it a lot, and I think you do, too."

The day I chose not to go on the nature walk, Gloria told me that Mrs. Kaplan wanted to see me.

I stood at her desk and waited as she read from my folder.

Finally, she looked up and smiled.

"We are told, Margaret, that today you were assigned to partner Berkeley Sims for our nature walk. Berkeley reported that you told her to tell Gloria that you preferred not to go." Mrs. Kaplan continued to smile, waiting for me to respond. No question had been asked, and she had not said anything that needed correcting, so I said nothing. At last, she asked an actual question. "Is this true, Margaret?"

"Yes."

Mrs. Kaplan closed the folder and pulled one of the camp brochures from the holder that was on the corner of her desk. She studied the picture on the front and asked, "Tell us, Margaret, did you and your parents read the camp brochures we sent?"

"Yes."

"Did you watch the video?"

"Yes."

"After reading the brochures and seeing the video, did you not choose Camp Talequa over all the others for the very reason that you *preferred* the activities at our camp?"

"Yes."

"So, Margaret, tell us why you refuse to participate."

I answered, "I prefer not to."

"Do you prefer not to tell us, or do you prefer not to participate?"

"Both."

Mrs. Kaplan's smile froze. She started to say my name but got only as far as the first syllable. Her upper lip would not move. Her teeth were parched. She ran her tongue over her teeth and said, "Now, Margaret, we want you to do something for us. We want you to get into the spirit of Camp Talequa." She trained her eyes on me before allowing another smile to visit her face. Her head bobbed forward and back, forward and back, forward and back in a rhythm that was either a lot of *yes*ses or an essential tremor, which is an idiopathic something that happens to seniors. She was either emphasizing something or showing her age. I watched and waited. She waited too. I think she was waiting for me to cry. I didn't.

At last she said, "Margaret, there are girls who come to this camp year after year after year. For some of them it is not just the best part of the summer, it is the best part of their whole year." Dry-eyed and silent, I watched her head bob—yes yes yes yes—like a toy dog on the back ledge of a pickup truck. To keep up the eye contact, my head oscillated, keeping time with her. Mrs. Kaplan thought I was not resonating but agreeing, so she said, "We want you to get to know those girls, Margaret. There are six of them right in your cabin." She looked down at my folder. "Meadowlark," she said. And the bobbing—yes yes yes yes—started again.

"It *is* Meadowlark, is it not, Margaret?" Of course it was Meadowlark. How else would she know that there were *six of them* in my cabin? To avoid a recurrence of the bobbing syndrome, and possible hypnosis, I avoided making eye contact and nodded, just once, a substantial yes. "Speak up," she insisted. "It is Meadowlark, is it not, Margaret?"

"Yes. I am in Meadowlark."

"Well, Margaret, there are in Meadowlark cabin six young ladies who have been to Camp Talequa every summer since they were ten years old."

"The Alums," I said matter-of-factly.

"Yes. There are six in your cabin. Let us give you their names—"

"I know who they are, Mrs. Kaplan."

Despite what I said, she continued to call roll: a beat, a name, a nod. "—Alicia Silver, Blair Patayani, Ashley—"

"—Schwartz, Kaitlin Lorenzo, Stacey Mouganis, and Heather Featherstone," I concluded.

The nodding stopped. I guessed that since she could start and stop it at will, it was not an essential tremor due to advanced age. Mrs. Kaplan said, "So you know who they are."

"Everybody does."

"Those girls are on the right track, Margaret. It would behoove you to get to know them. Do you understand what I mean?"

"I know what *behoove* means."

"It means we want you to become friends with those girls, Margaret. They will show you how to become a true participant in Camp Talequa." She put the brochure back in the holder, made sure the edges were even, and then asked, "Now, can you tell us what you do prefer?" She began oscillating yes yes yes yes again.

I watched, hypnotized.

"Can you tell us what you do want?"

When I answered, she sent me to the camp nurse for an evaluation.

I spent the entire nature walk afternoon in front of the mirror in the bathroom. I practiced facial expressions, putting on makeup, and doing things with my hair.

I decided that hair is destiny.

The other new girl, Berkeley Sims, had hair that was eager to please. She could blow it straight or let it dry curly. It even had two popular colors: brown streaked with blond. But given a choice, I would choose hair like Blair Patayani's. She had quiet but determined hair: long, straight, thick, and very black. My own hair was noisy. It was dark and thick, took hours to dry, and refused to be tied up, pinned down, braided, or twisted into a bun. It was always difficult to manage.

When my cabin mates returned from their nature walk, they rushed in to take showers. They went in two at a time, leaving Ashley for last. I heard her run her shower. I heard it shut off. And then I saw Ashley come running out. "The water is up to my ankles in there. It won't drain. Something's wrong."

Glaring at me, Kaitlin said, "I'll go get Gloria."

Gloria arrived, went into the bathroom, and a minute later came out and said, "Who did this?"

The girls shrugged. Alicia said, "When we came back, we all saw that one of the showers wasn't working, so we doubled up and used the other one."

Stacey added, "Ashley was last. We forgot to tell her the one on the right was stopped up."

Kaitlin said, "On the left."

Stacey blushed. "I meant the one on the left." She quickly added, "It was working last night. Something must have happened this afternoon when the rest of us were on our nature walk."

—friendly guidance

Glaring at me, Gloria said, "I'll get Jake to fix it."

four

We were miles past the camp when I asked Uncle Alex, "Do you think that Mrs. Kaplan has a narcissistic personality disorder?"

"Why do you ask?"

"Well, for one thing, a person who suffers from narcissistic personality disorder has a huge sense of self-importance, and Mrs. Kaplan must think she is so important that she is plural. She always says *we* for *I*. She does it all the time. There is no one else in the room, but it's '*we* ask,' '*we* require,' '*we* do not allow,' and '*we* want.' An awful lot of '*we* want.'"

Uncle chuckled. "I don't know about personality disorders, Margitkám. I only know about three kinds of *we*." He settled himself deeper into the car seat and inched himself around so that we better faced each other. "First," he said, "there is the real *we*—the plural—that means I plus others. Then there is the editorial *we*. News anchors say *we* a lot. They are speaking for themselves and others—their bosses at the station, I guess. And finally, there is the royal *we*. A queen will say,

'We are not amused.' That is Mrs. Kaplan. The woman thinks she is a queen, and you, my dear, are her loyal subject."

"*Wasn't,*" I insisted. "I wasn't loyal, and I wasn't her subject. I wasn't her predicate, either." Uncle laughed. He had a plump laugh—round and big-bellied. "I wasn't exactly obedient, but I wasn't exactly *dis*obedient, either. Not really. Like if someone does not agree with you, they *dis*agree with you. I was something in between being obedient and disobedient. If someone doesn't agree or disagree, what is she?"

"You were what I would call neutral. Like shifting gears in a car. When you put it in neutral, you can't go one way or the other—forward or backward. If you're in neutral, you stand still."

Uncle seemed to know more about driving cars than people who actually do. Even though I was familiar with the term *shifting gears* and knew what it meant, I had never actually seen anyone do it. I didn't know how Uncle knew about shifting gears, but I was not about to question him. I simply loved knowing that he understood. I said, "*That's* what I was. Standing still. Neither obeying nor disobeying."

"I think the word for what you were is *anobedient,* which would mean without obedience—which is not the same thing as *dis*obedience. I would say that anobedience is related to words like anesthetic, which means without feeling."

"Or anonymous, which means without a name."

"Or anorexia, without an appetite or anemia, without blood."

"Or Anne Boleyn, without a head."

Uncle laughed out loud.

I noticed Jake watching from the rearview mirror. I thought I caught him smiling, but I couldn't be sure because from where I sat, the mirror showed only half his face.

On the Sunday we were scheduled to go tubing on the lake, Gloria did a quick head count on the bus and realized that she was one camper short. She charged off the bus and headed for Meadowlark cabin, where she found me fully dressed, lying on my bunk, my head propped up by pillows, leaning against the wall, reading. Gloria told me that if I didn't hurry, the bus would leave without me, and I said that that was fine with me because I preferred not to go.

She took a deep breath. "You should have told me."

"I did. Last night when you were doing paperwork."

"I didn't hear."

"Or weren't listening."

Gloria reported me to Mrs. Kaplan, which led to some more

—friendly guidance

About an hour after the bus left, Mrs. Kaplan came into Meadowlark. She was carrying a plate of cookies and a container of milk.

She found me lying on my bunk, my arms under my head, my foot beating time to Michael Jackson's *Thriller* on my Walkman. I sat up as soon as she came in. She patted the edge of the lower bunk. "Come, Margaret," she said. "Come sit here so that we can have a little chat." She placed the plate of cookies between us. "Help yourself," she said.

I took a cookie and said thank you. The little chat went downhill from there.

Mrs. Kaplan seemed to take issue with everything I said until I said the one thing that made her so mad that she put an abrupt end to the little chat, and her smile dropped so fast, it almost made a sound. Her nostrils dilated, and she seemed to vacuum in half the air in the room. Huffing out the syllables of my name, she said, "Margaret Kane." She took a deep breath, this time sucking the air back in through her clenched teeth. "Margaret Kane, we want you to think about the cruel thing you have just said. We want you to think about that very hard. *Very* hard. And then we want you to think about what you can do to apologize."

She sprang up from the bed as if from a trampoline.

The paper plate fell, and the remaining cookie broke into a hundred pieces.

I sat on Heather's bunk, bouncing ever so slightly from the recoil of the mattress. Mrs. Kaplan looked down upon me and the scattered cookie with equal contempt. She said, "You may sweep that up." She paused just a second and added, "Now!" She watched as I got the broom and started sweeping. "When you've finished here, we would like you to report to the infirmary and see Ms. Starr. And we don't want to hear that you prefer not to."

Ms. Starr was Nurse Louise. I did not like her at all. Except for the fact that she dyed her hair and wore a lab coat, she was just like Mrs. Kaplan. I truly would have preferred not to go there again.

As soon as Mrs. Kaplan left, I began to sing:

"God save our gracious Queen
Long live our noble Queen
God save the Queen!"

I sang as I swept and by the time I had finished the fifth verse and had sung the second verse (my favorite) twice, I had swept the entire cabin from wall to wall, paying special attention to the four corners. When I was finished, I decided that "sweep that up" did not also mean "pick it up," so I left the mound of crumbs, dust bunnies, and sand in a neat pile at the entrance, propped the broom in a corner by the door, and left for the infirmary.

five

We were now on a part of the highway that is officially scenic. We were passing markers that explained—in paragraphs that were too long and lettering that was too small—what we should be appreciating. A person would have to be an extremely rapid reader or be in an extremely slow vehicle to be able to make out what they said. I didn't even try.

Tartufo sat on the floor, resting his head on the seat between Uncle and me. I stared out the window, thinking that everyone at Talequa had a name for me but none of them knew me. Even if I would never get a prize for being Miss Congeniality, I didn't deserve *incorrigible*.

"Nurse called me incorrigible, Uncle," I said.

Uncle lifted my hand and kissed my fingertips. It was an Old World thing he did when he approved of me—which was often. "I know," he said. "I read the report."

"I didn't know she wrote it, too."

By the time I got back to the cabin after seeing Nurse Louise, all the Meadowlarks had returned from tubing.

The first thing I noticed was that the mound of crumbs and dust balls at the threshold was gone, scattered back over the floor of the cabin. The second thing I noticed was that Ashley and Alicia looked incandescent. Then I saw that everyone had a neon glow. Even Blair Patayani, whose skin was a shade of coffee ice cream and who had bragged that she never burned, did. I made my way into the room. Everyone was oddly quiet. When I got to my bunk, I saw why.

One foot of my bunk ladder was sitting in an ugly pool of vomit. Heather Featherstone, who had the bunk beneath me, was lying on her side with her back to the room. Her back was a luminous shade of raspberry. She was clutching her Fringie to her stomach. I asked, "What happened?"

Berkeley Sims stepped forward and said, "Maybe you can tell us."

"What do you mean?"

Ashley exchanged a knowing smile with Berkeley before saying, "That mess was not here when we left, and you were the only one in the cabin."

I opened my mouth to answer, but I couldn't speak. I hopped over the lowest rung of the ladder and made my way up to my bunk, holding on to both rails of the ladder so that they could not see me shaking.

Looking like two low-wattage infrared bulbs, Alicia

and Blair came over. Stacey and Kaitlin joined them, and then, as if on some unspoken signal, the six of them formed a semicircle and stood shoulder to shoulder at the foot of the bed, giving as wide a berth to the pool of vomit as the space between the beds allowed. I don't know who said "Clean it up" first. Maybe it was Kaitlin, but it could have been Ashley. I looked around from face to face. They returned my stare, and in that brief exchange of looks, I saw it happen. I saw them change from nasty to vicious. Right before my eyes they closed in, silently at first. Then they linked arms at their shoulders, and with the precision of a line of Radio City Rockettes, they started chanting, "Clean it up, clean it up, clean it up."

I was no longer shaking. I was frozen in place. My blind inner self must have told me that they were beyond reason, beyond logic. Anything I could have said—had I been able to speak—would not convince them otherwise. I sat up there on my bed and watched them invent their rage. They had become a warrior gang. They needed a victim. Me.

They picked up a rhythm. "Clean it up, clean it up, clean it up, up, up."

In a groupthink pause between chants, Gloria came in.

They shut up and quickly dropped arms.

Gloria assumed the girls were gathered around my bunk out of concern for Heather. "How is she?" she asked. The girls broke up to let Gloria through. She sidestepped the base of the ladder and sat down on the edge of Heather's bed, just where Mrs. Kaplan had sat earlier. She said, "Jake's over in the mess hall. Why don't one of you go tell him what happened. He'll know what to do."

Ashley volunteered to go, but not before exchanging a vile smile with Kaitlin and Alicia.

That evening when Gloria came back to the cabin, I sat up in my bunk and sang "God Save the Queen." I sang all five verses all the way through and then sang them all the way through again.

I was looking out the window, but I was seeing nothing. I was thinking about the three kinds of *we*: The plural *we*, the editorial *we*, and the royal *we*. I could thank my id, the part of my psyche that is totally unconscious, for knowing that Mrs. Kaplan thought she was a queen. My subconscious knew even before I did that the woman thinks she is a royal *we*. It was my id that instinctively chose "God Save the Queen" as the song I should sing. I started to hum it.

Uncle asked, "What are you singing, Margitkám?"

"The same song that I sang yesterday."

"What song was that?"

"The British national anthem. I started singing it yesterday afternoon. Later, I sang it sitting up in my bunk."

"Always the same song?"

"Always 'God Save the Queen.'" In a weak tremolo I began:

> *"God save our gracious Queen,*
> *Long live our noble Queen,*
> *God save the Queen!*
> *Send her victorious,*
> *Happy and glorious,*
> *Long to reign over us;*
> *God save the Queen!"*

"Where did you learn that?"

"Sixth grade. My language arts teacher was an Anglophile. She made us learn five verses. She said there was a sixth, but she didn't like it, so we only learned five. Listen to the second verse. It's my favorite."

> *"O Lord our God arise,*
> *Scatter her enemies*
> *And make them fall,*
> *Confound their politics,*

Frustrate their knavish tricks,
On Thee our hopes we fix,
God save us all!"

Uncle laughed. "Very good," he said. "And very appropriate."

I sang the second verse again, and soon Uncle started humming. By the time I got to the top again, he was singing along. Neither of us had any singing voice to speak of, and Tartufo reacted by lifting his head and howling.

Uncle asked, "What happened when you sang, Margitkám?"

"Nothing. The Meadowlarks paid no attention at all. I think it's called 'shunning.' All of them except Gloria, my counselor."

"What did Gloria do?"

"At first she tried to ignore me, but after I had sung it straight through for a second time, she asked me to please stop. *'Please, Margaret, please stop singing that song,'* she said."

"And what did you do?"

"I stopped singing, and I started to hum. I hummed. I hummed and hummed until I came to *Frustrate their knavish tricks.* I sang those words, and then I *la, la, la, la, la*ed, until I came to *God save us all!* I sang those words, and then I started humming again. Do you think I was being incorrigible?"

"Incorrigible? I'm not so sure. But irritating, yes. Irritating, I'm very sure."

"Good," I said, strangely satisfied. And then, as if prompted by a choral director, we sang the first two verses all over again. This time Tartufo lifted his head and howled as if the moon and not the sun were full and visible. We stopped after singing a second chorus, and Uncle Alex kissed the top of Tartufo's head, and I did too, and that was the moment when I caught Jake the handyman's reflection in the rearview mirror, and this time—no mistake about it—he was smiling. Definitely smiling.

At last we came to highway signs that were big enough to read, and they said that we were approaching a rest area. Uncle leaned forward and asked the driver to please stop.

"No problem."

Uncle replied, "My two favorite words," and then he added, *"köszönöm szépen,"* his Old World thank you.

Just before he put on his turn signal to change lanes, Jake the handyman turned half around and smiled directly at me. His smile was slightly mischievous and totally unvarnished.

six

When I came out of the rest room, Jake was standing in front of the car, holding Tartufo's leash, smoking a cigar. No genuine fragile X person could smoke a cigar and look relaxed at the same time.

"If it's all right with you, I'll give Tartufo a little run," I said.

He handed me the leash. "Take your time," he said. "No hurry." He flicked the ash from his cigar with a smooth gesture. I started toward a sign that pointed to a dog run in the back of the rest area, and glanced back at Jake. He was leaning against the car hood, a faint, relaxed smile on his face. An Asperger's wouldn't be leaning nonchalantly against the car hood; he'd be banging his head against it. I wondered if there were two handymen named Jake at Camp Talequa. One normal; one not.

Tartufo took his time about where to lift his leg, and when I returned to the car, I found Uncle and Jake deep in conversation. Tartufo lunged toward Uncle, yipping with excitement as if he had not seen him for days. I wondered how dogs measure time. Do they multiply minutes by seven, the way I did at Camp Talequa?

I turned the leash over to Uncle and started to open the back door of the car when Jake, between puffs of relighting his cigar, said, "No hurry."

Who was this man who looked and sounded as if he not only knew what was going on but was in charge?

Then Uncle said, "That accident on the highway really slowed us down."

Jake caught on right away. He took a deep pull on the cigar, then held it at arm's length and twirled it between his thumb and forefinger while examining it. "Three cars," he declared. He smiled slyly in the direction of the highway, where cars were zipping by at the speed of sound. "People on the scene said that the ambulance was delayed by heavy traffic." He carefully snuffed out his cigar on the sole of his shoe, checked that it was cool, and slipped the rest of it into the bib pocket of his coveralls, which he buttoned closed.

Uncle looked over the six lanes of moving vehicles. "Traffic backed up for hours. . . ."

"It wasn't easy getting the lifeflight helicopter to land at the site of the accident," Jake said as he reached into the front seat of the car and took out a cooler. "Witnesses say that people delayed by the massive traffic jam were led to the best table by a man who was familiar with the territory and that they shared their loaves and tuna fishes." He smiled again. "Follow me."

We assembled around the table that he led us to. After we were seated, I asked if he had a last name.

"Kaplan," he replied. "I am Jacob Kaplan."

"Are you her husband?" I asked, shocked.

"Her son."

Uncle said, "That makes you the heir apparent."

Jake laughed. "Only in a technical sense. It is true that I am the son of the reigning queen, but I am nothing more than an obedient subject."

I looked at Uncle, and he looked at me, and as if on cue, we chorused, "Anobedient subject? Are you *anobedient?*"

Jake shook his head no and then nodded yes and laughed. "I guess I am."

We ate slowly, enjoying the shade and the slight breeze that floated across the highway. Jake told us that he had become his mother's handyman when he lost his job as a billboard painter. "After so many states passed laws forbidding billboards, especially the big ones like the ones I painted, I was out of work. Mother needed a handyman, and I needed a job. I am a better painter than I am a handyman. But what good is being good at a craft no one wants?"

Uncle Alex replied, "My brother is in a similar situation."

"Is he a billboard painter?"

"No, he is a watchmaker. Not quite as bad because there are still some watches that don't run on batteries, and people still need repairs. My brother, too, is good at his craft. He is expert at doing fine-tuning and repair work on what he calls *timepieces*, by which he means clocks and watches that have gears and springs. We have a place—a kiosk—in the Fivemile Creek Mall."

Jake Kaplan looked at me and winked. "Sooner or later, we all do what we have to do—even if it means fixing plumbing."

Uncle and Jake gathered up the wrappings from lunch and walked toward the trash barrel by the side of the walkway. I followed, holding Tartufo's leash. After they dumped the trash, I gave the leash to Uncle and then hung back. I was so happy not to be programmed for walks/talks/arts/crafts that I felt as if I had been given a hall pass. Freer than that. Freer even than the last day of school. I was *excused*.

No more Meadowlarks.

What a relief!

No more powdered-milk breakfasts.

What a relief!

No more crafts-on-demand or Mother Nature. No

more friendly guidance from experienced counselors. No more, no more, no more.

I spread my arms eagle-wing wide, then with my fingers splayed, I slowly raised my arms as high as I could, and lifted my face to the sky where I directed my thanks. I would soon be at my uncles' house. I would soon be hanging out. I would soon be in the Tower Garden. I would soon be eating while the Meadowlarks had lights-out. "Yes!" I yelled. "Yes, yes, yes." I dropped my arms to my sides and twirled around three times— three times to totally cast out the Doom of Talequa.

Then I ran to catch up with Uncle and Jake.

As we walked to the car, Uncle said, "May I suggest, Mr. Kaplan, that when your car breaks down in Epiphany, you join us for dinner?"

Jacob Kaplan said, "I would like that very much."

Uncle Alex asked, "Can you tell me whether your mother will be pleased or angry when she discovers that there won't be an auto repair bill?"

Jacob beamed two bright eyes directly at me and said, "I prefer not to."

seven

Uncle Morris was sitting on the top step of the service porch, waiting.

As soon as Jake cut the motor, I was out of the car, and before I was halfway across the yard, I was in his arms. He squeezed me to him, and there in the welcome of those arms I felt right about myself for the first time in more than a week.

Uncle Morris Rose was five inches taller than his brother, and although he weighed just as much, the pounds spread out over those five extra inches made him look formidable rather than jolly. He was as bald as Uncle Alex, but Uncle Morris resented it, so he parted his hair an inch above his left ear and combed a few stray strands over the top of his head, his comb-over. He further compensated for the lack of hair on his head by wearing a commanding mustache; Alex was clean-shaven. Morris was three years older and six years bossier. His Hungarian accent was deeper, his syntax more foreign, his manner gruffer, his temper shorter, his eyesight better, his hearing worse.

The three Rose siblings had emigrated from Hungary together: Alexander, Morris, and Margaret, their sister and my grandmother, who died the year before I was born. Margaret was the oldest, and her brothers had loved her very much, and for all their differences, large and small, there was nothing they agreed on more than this: I, Margaret Rose, was their sister's name made flesh, and they loved me *an*endingly.

Even after Uncle Morris released me from his big bear hug, Jake still had not stepped inside the open gate. He stood stock-still between the car door and the iron pipe fence and stared. Uncle Alex beckoned to him to come forward and be introduced to his brother.

"Can it wait a minute?" he begged. "I want to look. Let me look. Just look."

Pleased—how could he not be?—by Jacob's reaction to the towers, Uncle Morris called back, "Take your time. Help yourself."

Uncle Alex said, "Jacob will be joining us for dinner."

Glancing back at Jake, Uncle Morris said, "Certainly," and then he urged me, "Inside, *édes* Margitkám. Come inside." He swung the screen door wide and let me pass in front of him. "Tell me, what did they do to you?"

"It was me, Uncle. It was what I did," I replied. I

took a step back and said, "I did nothing. That was the problem." I laughed, and Uncle laughed too.

As soon as Uncle Alex came inside and closed the screen door behind him, Uncle Morris said, "I see you brought Tartufo." To which Alex replied, "No, Morris, this is my *other* dog. My spare."

"As ugly as your first."

Morris Rose did not approve of Tartufo. He complained about the hair he shed. He complained about the smell of the big sack of dog food that Uncle Alex kept in the corner of the service porch and the bowl of water on the floor next to it, which he managed to kick over at least once a week.

"Who's minding the store?" Uncle Alex asked.

"Who do you think?"

"Is it Helga?"

"Of course it's Helga," Morris replied. "I requested her."

"So then it's all right."

"What do you mean, *then it's all right*? Is it all right because she doesn't steal, or is it all right because she makes fewer mistakes than the other one?"

Uncle Alex asked, "Which other one?"

"The one you like."

"I like them all."

Holding his hands to the sides of his head, Uncle

Morris said to the kitchen table. "*Jaj, Istenem!* He likes them all. He likes them all because they apologize when they make a mistake."

Uncle Alex asked, "Which other one do I like?"

"The boy."

"Why didn't you say *the boy*? If you had said *the boy*, I'd know which is *the other one.*"

Exasperated, Uncle Morris waved his open palms. "So if you know which is the other one, who is it?"

"It's the boy with the tattoo on his wrist."

"Of course," Uncle Morris insisted. "I told you it's the one you like."

"So what's his name?" Uncle Alex asked.

"Which one? The one you like?"

Now it was Uncle Alex's turn to be exasperated. "I like them all. Who's the one with the tattoo?"

Uncle Morris held his hands to his head again. This time he addressed the ceiling. "The tattoo is Dennis." He repeated, "It's Dennis."

"So why didn't you say Dennis?" Alex asked.

"Because he's not there," Morris answered.

"No, Helga is. That's what you said when I asked."

Uncle Morris shrugged and told the kitchen table, "He asks. I answer. He asks again. I answer again."

Uncle Alex waved his hand in front of his face and told the nearest chair, "He has all the answers. Always he has answers. Even if there is no question, my brother has answers." Then he whistled for Tartufo and filled his dish with fresh water.

I was so happy to hear my uncles argue, I practically floated up the stairs to stash my gear. My room was the small one in the back. It had a window that overlooked the towers.

I could see Jake from my bedroom window. He walked all around the Tower Garden and then all around again. He walked around each of the towers before he stepped inside Tower Two, the tallest one, the one just outside my bedroom window. He stood inside the circle of ribs and struts and looked up and up for a long, long time. As he ducked under its lowest rungs he grazed a few of the hanging glass ornaments. I saw him start to count the pendants on a single rung, but he stopped, stepped back, and looked. Just looked. Like a kiss or a walk in the woods, the towers were meant to be experienced, not inventoried.

He walked the length of the pathway between the flowers and the towers twice before sitting down on the back porch step. That's where he was when I came downstairs and joined him.

Inside the Crypto-Cabin

eight

Not then, but when the events of that summer were history, Jake explained how he had come to be the one to drive Uncle and me back to Epiphany.

Jake had an arrangement with his mother. When Camp Talequa was in session—as well as in the spring and the fall, when Mrs. Kaplan rented the facilities to Elderhostel—Jake took care of maintenance. In winter, after all the sessions were over, and the camp was empty, Jake stayed on. He drained the water pipes and cleared heavy snow from the cabin roofs. In exchange for these services, he had year-round use of a small cabin that was deep into the woods that bordered the campgrounds. He liked to keep its location secret from all the campers, young and old.

Acting stupid was a pose he had chosen when he first took the job. He knew all too well how easily young girls could interpret a smile as sexy or sinister, and how easily a greeting—as simple as a hello—could be interpreted as a come-on. So he made a policy of not responding to anything they said, anything they did. The easiest way to do that was to act as if he had an IQ between vegetable and mineral. He didn't call anyone by name, didn't talk to anyone, and pretended he didn't understand when they whispered and giggled about him. But he saw a lot and heard a lot. And he knew all the camp tricks.

His mother was as anxious as he was to keep the location of his little house in the big woods a secret. She seldom came.

The first time she visited Jake's cabin that year I was at Talequa was in the evening after I had preferred not to go on the nature walk, the day of our first little talk. It was well past the dinner hour when she made her way from her office to her son's secret cabin.

When she was sitting behind her camp director's desk, Mrs. Kaplan wore camp shirts with epaulets, stiff with starch, neatly tucked into the waistband of her chinos—either slacks or skirt. For her off-duty trip to her son's house that evening, she wore a long skirt made of wispy material, a large chunky necklace made of bone and bronze, and Birkenstocks. For camouflage as well as for protection against the cool evening air, she had wrapped herself in a darkly embroidered silk shawl bordered with a deep fringe.

She opened the front door slowly and averted her eyes.

The front room of his secret cabin was uncarpeted and largely occupied by two easels, on each of which was an unfinished painting. Regardless of the size of the canvas, Jake painted large. His unframed canvases of hips and lips, breasts and thighs—painted in flesh colors but shaded in brilliant hues of alizarin crimson and dioxazine purple—leaned, three- or four-deep, on all sides of the room.

Mrs. Kaplan loved Jake, but there were times when she felt that she did not get the son she deserved. She did not approve of his style of housekeeping or his keeping a pot of coffee plugged in when he was not at home—even though he knew she disapproved of keeping things plugged in, switched on, or left running. She also did not care for his style of painting or his subject matter. At best, she thought his canvases looked like illustrations for a catalog of organ transplants. She found them embarrassing—just a half beat short of pornography.

But worst of all, she had a son who had an attitude about her attitudes. He called the Talequa handbook "The Kaplan Manifesto."

Jake watched his mother unfurl the shawl from her shoulders and toss it over the back of the lone upholstered chair in his front room. She cleared the magazines and newspapers from the seat and stacked them neatly on the floor. She sank into the chair and extended her arms over the length of the padded arm-rests, her fingers gripping the edges. She settled back into the chair and, after checking it for grease, carefully placed her head against the back cushion. He saw that despite the Birkenstocks and despite the unfurled shawl, his mother was as wound up and as stiff as a spool of nylon filament.

He offered her a cup of coffee. She refused. She took a deep breath, inhaling fumes of turpentine, cigar smoke, and motes of dust. She coughed—a little more than was necessary to clear her throat—and said, "How can you stand the smells in this room?"

"Keeps the mosquitoes away," he said casually.

Not the answer she wanted to hear.

Jake knew that with limited means and limited education, his mother had done her best when his father had walked out on them. Jake knew that his mother had a tendency to mistake rules, her rules, for principles. She did not bend because she did not have enough confidence to know when or how far. She did not listen well because one ear was always otherwise engaged—either listening to what she herself had just said or what she would say next.

Jake believed that when his father left, his mother lit a small flame of displeasure deep inside herself. For a long time he thought that if that pilot light ever went out, she would die. Sometimes when he aggravated her—which he almost always did—he consoled himself by telling himself that he was feeding the little flame that kept her alive. That evening, however, it was obvious that she was more upset than usual. The tiny jet of displeasure was already burning brightly, and he did not need to feed the flame.

He poured himself a cup of coffee and carefully added cream—real cream—until the color was the exact shade of raw umber he wanted. He added two teaspoons of sugar and slowly stirred. He took a long sip, savoring the taste and the aroma. He resisted the temptation to smoke a cigar because if he lit up, his mother would explode and leave without telling him what was on her mind. And he knew that she would never have risked a trip to his cabin unless something serious had come up. He was curious. He wanted to hear what it was. "Is something the matter, Mother?" he asked.

She did not look directly at him. "I am having a problem with one of our campers. Refuses to do anything. When asked why, she says, 'I prefer not to.'"

"Bartleby," Jake said.

"What's that? Bartleby?"

"'Bartleby the Scrivener.' It's a story by Herman Melville. This lawyer, whose name we never learn, hires a copyist, a *scrivener*, a man who writes out duplicate copies of legal documents. That's what they did before they had carbon paper or copy machines. To check for accuracy, one man reads out loud from the original, and the scriveners check their copies, word for word, against what is being read. Thus the term *copyreader*. When the lawyer asks Bartleby to check his copy against a reading of the original, Bartleby says, 'I would prefer not to.' As the story goes on, there is more and more that Bartleby prefers not to do. The strange thing is, the lawyer who hired him, and whom we suspect is partly Melville himself, is sympathetic to Bartleby."

"Perhaps that lawyer could afford to be sympathetic, but I cannot." She sighed wearily. "There is something more about this child that I can't put my finger on. I've had this camp long enough to have seen it all. I've had girls who yell and scream about the food and the accommodations and their cabin mates. And I've *heard* it all as well. I've had girls come into the office cursing and swearing, and I can tell you, Jake, you would be surprised at the extensive vocabulary of bad, very bad, *hyphenated*-bad words that some of these girls have."

Jake smiled at the thought of his mother having to listen to bad, very bad, hyphenated-bad words.

"Why are you smiling?" she asked.

"Was I smiling?"

"You most certainly were."

"Was it my idiot smile or a smirk?"

"It was—" She stopped short. "Now, don't ask me to analyze your smiles. It was a smile pure and simple."

"Pure and simple. So it was my idiot smile after all."

"We don't say *idiot* anymore, Jacob. Nobody's an idiot anymore."

"Nobody's an idiot, or nobody *says* idiot?" One quick look told him that she was within an inch of taking the bait. "I'm interested, Mother," he said. "I really am. Please tell your pure and simple son what is on your mind."

"This Bartleby camper is on my mind."

"What did she do?"

"That's what I'm trying to tell you. She doesn't *do* anything. She—"

"Yes, yes. She prefers not to."

"I called her in for an interview today."

"Did she cry?"

"No, she didn't cry. I've had girls who cry. I know what to do when that happens."

Actually, his mother liked it best when the girls

broke down and cried. She offered Kleenex and comfort, in that order, and then she thanked the girl for sharing her feelings. Then, with her thumb, she would gently lift the girl's chin and ask her "to give us another chance." It was always a masterful performance.

"If she didn't cry, did she at least tell you that she wanted to go home?"

"Oh, she didn't say she wanted to go home."

"What did she say?"

"When I asked her to tell me what she did want, she said . . ." His mother could not finish the sentence. She looked down at the floor at some old cigar ash and began rubbing it into the floorboards with her Birkenstock. When she looked up, she opened her mouth to speak but couldn't.

"What did she say? It'll be better if you tell me."

His mother studied the floor again and found a bit of cigar ash that had escaped and began rubbing it into the grain of the wood. She swallowed hard. Still not looking at her son, she answered, "When I asked her what she did want, she said, 'I want this interview to be over.'"

This time, Jake lowered his head so that his mother could not see the smile that seemed to have taken up residence on his face. This Bartleby was amusing him as much as she was annoying his mother. When he was certain that he had banished the last trace of a smile, he gently teased his mother by saying, "I'll bet you told her that there are girls who come here every year. . . ."

His mother, deaf to his playfulness, replied, "I most certainly did tell her that."

Still teasing, Jake continued, ". . . and for them Camp Talequa is the best part of the summer. . . ."

"I am very proud of that."

"And did you tell her that you wanted her to get to know those girls?"

"Of course I did. I told her that there are six alums in her cabin, Meadowlark. . . ."

"Mother!" he exclaimed. "You didn't! You didn't put that single outsider in with those six girls who insisted on rooming together."

"They made bunking together a condition of coming to camp."

"So, Mother, why didn't you give them a cabin to themselves?"

"And waste a two-bed space? There are *two* odd girls in that cabin. This *Bartleby* one is not alone. The other odd one seems to have made the adjustment."

"The very fact that you call her *the other odd one* should tell you a lot."

"And do I need to tell you how short the camping season is? Do I need to tell you that it is necessary for me to use every bed I have in order to turn a profit? You know perfectly well that there's one malcontent in every session. Besides, as you well know, complaints about cabin mates rank above all the others: the food, the activities, the counselors, the mosquitoes. But this Margaret—"

"Did you say this child's name is Margaret?"

His mother nodded. "Yes. Margaret Kane. Margaret Rose Kane, as she likes to remind everyone."

"Is that *Kane* with a *K*?" he asked.

"It is," she replied. Then, catching a look in his eye, she asked anxiously, "Why? What about her?"

Jake remembered being called to Meadowlark cabin when the girls came back from their nature walk. When Gloria told him that there was a problem with a shower drain there, he knew that he would pull a labeled T-shirt and/or underpants out of the pipe. He knew that whichever it would be, it would be clearly labeled. This time it was two T-shirts. Both name tags said M. R. KANE. He had hung the shirts over the door of the shower stall and left. As he was leaving, he heard the girls giggling. When he was only halfway out the door, he heard, "I'm not sure he can read." He was well out the door and into the dark of the woods before he risked blowing his cover and smiling to himself.

He also remembered changing a bunk mattress in the same cabin. Now he realized whose mattress it was. He should have paid more attention to the arrangements in that cabin. Six Alums, two outsiders: Not a good thing.

Jake asked, "You say this Margaret has no complaints about her cabin mates?"

"Not once. I repeat: Not once."

"Or is it *not once* that she's told you?"

"Despite what you may think, Jake, despite what you may want to believe, the Alums are not causing the problem." When Jake did not reply, she hastily added, "You must admit that I've had quite a bit of experience with preadolescent girls, and I am probably the last person on earth to label children—"

"Of course, Mother. *Labels* are right up there with *idiot*. Never to leave the tip of your tongue."

"That's right. But as I was saying, as much as I hate labeling children, as seldom as I find it necessary to do so, I must say that this child has exhibited all the classic symptoms of a passive-aggressive personality disorder."

He protested. "Mother, when a child says 'I want this interview to be over,' that does not sound passive to me, and 'I prefer not to' does not sound aggressive."

"However, Jacob, despite my distaste for labels, I do believe that this Bartleby—as you refer to her—is a textbook case of passive-aggressive personality disorder. Literally, a textbook case."

"How can you say that about a twelve-year-old?"

"This child's mother is a full professor of psychology at Clarion State University, and the child herself is an advanced reader. I wouldn't be at all surprised to find out that she's read that 'Bartleby' story."

"I was in college when I read it, Mother."

"Kids who grow up in a university grow up very fast. Faster than most. And it wouldn't surprise me to find her taking instructions on passive-aggressive behavior right out of one of her mother's psychology textbooks."

"Mother, listen to me, I don't want to hurt your feelings, but I think you'd be wise to drop your passive-aggressive analysis."

"Even if you don't agree with me, the camp nurse does."

"Oh, Mother!" he exclaimed. "Are you talking about Louise Starr?"

"I most certainly am."

"What does that great authority on child behavior conclude about our Bartleby?" Even though he wanted to keep his voice level, he could hear for himself that it had an edge.

"She reported that the child is simply uncooperative. *Simply uncooperative* is just an old-fashioned way of saying *passive-aggressive*." Jake shook his head. "It seems to me, Jake, that like that Bartleby lawyer, you are a little sympathetic to this camper, this Margaret Kane."

"No, Mother," Jake replied, "I would say that I am a lot sympathetic to her." His mother picked up her shawl, wrapped it around herself, and left the cabin without saying another word.

There! He had done it. Despite wanting to be sympathetic, despite not wanting to fan the flame of her anger, he had done it. But he was angry, too. Alums: six; outsiders: two. Greed should stop where good judgment begins.

On the day that Uncle Alex negotiated a ride back to Epiphany, Mrs. Kaplan had assigned one of the kitchen staff to do the driving. But Jake, who had been doing cleanup around the office cabin and had overheard the greater part of his mother's conversation with Uncle Alex, had insisted that it be he.

The Towers and the Town

nine

Jake and I sat together on the back steps. We looked, just looked, for a long time. Then I said, "This is where I wanted to stay while my parents are in Peru."

Jake replied, "I can understand that. I would want to stay here too."

It was the time of year when the big-bellied, lantern-shaped peppers hung heavily on their stems and bent them low. "Uncle Morris grows the peppers," I said, "and Uncle Alex grows the roses."

"And the towers? Who did the towers?"

"Both of them. They've been building them for forty-five years. They are older than my mother." I pointed to the space that zagged between the third tower and the fence and said, "There's room for a fourth." Jake squinted and shielded his eyes to look in the direction I pointed. "It will be tall and slender so that it will fit in the space." He studied the spot as if to visualize another tower. "Many of the pieces are ready. They're in their basement workroom."

Jake's focus shifted up and down and slowly around, but he didn't take his eyes off the towers. Not even once. He rested his elbows on his thighs and folded his hands in front of him as if in prayer. He concentrated on the tower closest to the back porch steps. "What about the pendants?"

"Uncle Alex does those. He uses a grindstone to shape the pieces and a little drill to make the holes for the copper wire to fasten them. Uncle Morris drills the holes through the pipes where they're to be hung. They never discuss what they are going to do. They just argue over it. Every single piece. Uncle Morris asks, 'You want it here?' And he'll point. Uncle Alex will step back and look squinty-eyed at what Uncle Morris is point- ing to, and he'll say, 'No, here,' and he'll point to a spot that is an eighth of an inch away. 'You want it here?' Uncle Morris will say. 'Isn't that what I said?' Uncle Alex will answer. 'Are you sure? Because once I drill this hole, I can't *un*drill it.' Then Uncle Alex will step back again and say, 'If you're going to be so unsure, let me think about it.' 'I'm not unsure, *you're* the one who's unsure.' Uncle Morris will throw up his hands and say, *'Jaj, Istenem!'* which means *Oh, my God,* which he says a lot. They're always fighting. The Uncles have been liv- ing together for as long as I've known them, which is all my life, and they've been arguing ever since. My mother says it's worth the price of an opera ticket to watch them on pendant-hanging day. She loves the towers. So do I."

"Only a dead soul wouldn't," he said.

"Then that would be my father," I said.

Jake was embarrassed. "I didn't mean . . ."

"That's all right," I said. "My father and the Uncles have issues."

My father thought that building the towers with clock faces that didn't tell time was a waste of it. He was as relieved as I was hurt that my uncles did not put up an argument for my staying with them. He worried that if I lived with them for four weeks, I would never again remember to turn off the lights when I left a room and would never again be on time. He complained that they couldn't keep track of keys, bills, appointments, or time. Especially time. Being on time was a religion to Father.

My father spoke of time as a conception, and the only definition of *conception* I knew meant that time was something he had fathered. He was my father, and he was also Father Time. He worried about wasting time and running out of time. Mostly, he worried about losing time. When I was little, I used to think that someday I would find a picture of his lost child Time on a milk carton. To Father, time was meant to be saved. He saved time all the time. He never said what he did with all the time he saved, but no one ever asked because people always admire people who save time.

To the Uncles, time was meant to be spent.

When people asked my father—and I hated when they did—what he thought of the towers, he would say that they were not only "useless, superfluous, a supreme waste of time," but also "an extravagant waste of money."

My mother's attitude was: "Extravagant? Yes, the towers are extravagant, but that hardly makes them a waste of money. Every now and then, a person must do something simply because he wants to, because it seems to him worth doing. And that does not make it worthless or a waste of time. It's true, the towers have no function. They do not give shelter. Neither does the statue of David. They don't hold up telephone wires. Neither does the Eiffel Tower. And the rose windows of Notre Dame don't let in enough light to read fine print. But by my definition, that doesn't make them useless or superfluous either. The towers are there simply because they are worth doing. Without them, my world would be less beautiful and a lot less fun."

A lingering sense of loyalty to my father kept me from telling Jake all of that. Instead, I asked, "Jake, have you ever seen the rose windows of Notre Dame?"

"No, I haven't."

"They're glass, aren't they?"

"Yes. Windows usually are."

Windows usually are. Of course windows are glass. Embarrassed beyond words, I studied Jacob Kaplan because now that I was sure that he had neither Asperger's nor fragile X, I wondered if he had a problem with sarcasm. Chronic sarcasm could be the symptom of a syndrome—even though I didn't know the name for that syndrome—if there was a name, if there was a syndrome.

The next thing Jake said was, "I've seen pictures of the rose windows of Notre Dame in my art history courses."

He wasn't being sarcastic. Not at all! "I've always dreamed of having a window of a rose," I confessed.

"It's not a window of a rose," he explained. "The traceries, the ornamental stonework that holds the colored glass in place, radiate out from a center circle like the petals of an open rose. That's why they're called rose windows."

"If the colored glass isn't a rose, what is it?"

"At Notre Dame, one of the big rose windows has a picture of the Virgin in the center. Notre Dame means *Our Lady.* As I understand it, she is encircled by figures from the Old Testament."

I thought about that. I said, "The figures from the Old Testament would be all right, but Our Lady wouldn't be. My uncles are Jewish."

"So is my father," Jake said.

"Oh, really?" I said. "I'm just the opposite. I have a Jewish mother and a Presbyterian father."

"Well," Jake replied, "I wouldn't say we're *opposite*. We're both half-and-half. I'd say that we are mirror images."

That remark made me very happy, and I didn't want to add anything to it, so I didn't. Instead, I told him, "I thought that the rose windows were windows of a rose. That's what I've always wanted: a window of a rose. Rose is my middle name."

"I know."

"It is also my uncles' last name."

"I know."

"My uncles never had children, and they don't want Rose to die."

"Neither do I," he said. He said nothing more for a minute. He studied the towers, and then he turned to me and said, "You could have a rose ceiling, Margaret."

I had heard about glass ceilings. They were what women in the workplace had to break through. "You don't mean glass, do you?"

"Not glass, Margaret. Paint. I could paint a rose on

your ceiling. One giant rose to cover your whole ceiling. The way I used to paint billboards."

I sighed deeply and said, "A rose rose ceiling is exactly what I've always wished for."

"Then you will have it," he said emphatically. "Rose rose it will be. It will be painted in multiple shades of passionate rose."

Multiple shades of passionate rose. That was even more than I had hoped for.

"But I will need a scaffold."

I said, "My uncles will make you one. They have enough pipe in the basement to make any kind you want." I knew without asking that if I asked my uncles to make a scaffold so that I could hang the moon, their only reservation would be that they believed that I had hung it already.

"I'll start on it this week. Wednesday is my day off. I'll come every Wednesday until it's done."

I said, "I'd hate for you to give up your day off for this." I, of course, did not at all hate the idea of his giving up his day off to come to Schuyler Place to paint my ceiling. I loved it.

Jake replied, "I won't be giving it up, I'll be filling it up."

I wanted to throw my arms around him and kiss him, and I would have if I had not wanted to so badly.

ten

We ate in the kitchen. For as long as I could remember, the Uncles had never dined in their dining room, so the four of us crowded around an old enamel-top table. We sat on wooden folding chairs that had not been manufactured since the invention of plastic. The slats were scratched, and their color had mellowed beyond yellow to mustard. But there was a linen cloth on the table. The napkins were linen too. The dishes were china; the glasses, crystal; and the silverware was sterling. The food was served family-style from antique tureens and platters and presented with a panache that would have been the pride of any four-star restaurant in Epiphany—if Epiphany had had a four-star restaurant.

Jake could hardly wait to find out more about the towers. He started by asking when they got started.

Morris was pleased that he had asked *when* and not *why.* There was no *why.* "It was a long time ago," he said. "I started shortly after we bought the house."

"It was a Glass house," Uncle Alex added.

"A glass house made of wood?" Jake asked.

"A Glass house because it was built by the Tappan Glass Works."

Uncle Morris said, "I didn't hear this man ask you who built the house. I thought I heard him ask *when* did we start the towers."

Looking sheepish, Uncle Alex answered, "He did. He asked *when*."

"Can I continue?"

"You can, and you may."

"So, if I *may*," Uncle Morris said, casting fish-eyes at his brother. "I started shortly after we moved into the house. Wilma, my wife, had died. I wanted to do something. I didn't even know what. I just knew it was not going to be small like a watch or exact like a clock. So one day I started. What I was building, I wasn't sure. An idea I had, but not a plan; so even before I decided what it was I was doing, I found out. I was building towers. They became as they grew."

—the Glass house

Like every other house in the neighborhood, the house at 19 Schuyler Place had been built and owned by the Tappan Glass Works. The company rented them to its workers until the factory was moved to the other side of the lake. Then the houses were sold. Like the Uncles, most of the people who bought them were immigrants to whom owning a home meant owning a piece of America.

Every house was tall and narrow and faced the street straight on. Every house had a front porch with four steps leading up to it, a mailbox nailed to the wall by the front door, and a metal box that sat on the floor of the porch near the steps. Milkmen delivered milk in glass bottles into the metal boxes, and mailmen carried heavy leather pouches that they lightened, one letter at a time, as they walked up and then down each flight of front porch steps.

The neighbors helped each other out in the small ways that neighbors can and the ways that friendly ones do. They held keys to each others' houses, and borrowed cups of sugar and shared cookies, casseroles, and the produce from their gardens.

They called each other "Mr." and "Mrs."

Mr. and Mrs. Bevilaqua lived at 17 Schuyler Place, and Mr. and Mrs. Vanderwaal lived at number 21.

Alex said, "We had once a jewelry store downtown, only one block away from Town Square. We called our store Jewels Bi-Rose. We loved the name. *Bi* was a play on English words. *B-I* means *two* and is also a homo-nym for *buy, B-U-Y,* and for *B-Y.*"

Morris pointed his chin in his brother's direction. "That one took care of the crystal and china. We had a bridal registry. I took care of the fine jewelry and watches."

Alex added, "Business at Jewels Bi-Rose was very personal. Half the diamond engagement rings and place settings of china sold in Epiphany came from Jewels Bi-Rose. That's the way it was before the days of discount stores and universal credit cards. Things were personal. If a customer wasn't satisfied with something, he complained to us, not to his lawyer. People who were our friends and neighbors were also our customers. Back then, when we had our store, one person could be all three—a friend, a neighbor, and a customer."

"Downtown was booming," Uncle Morris said.

"Business at Jewels Bi-Rose was good. Very good. Morris kept a watch repair shop in the back of Jewels Bi-Rose. People from all over Clarion County came to him to get their watches repaired. And then there were the clocks."

"I repaired the big clocks," Morris explained. "The ones that were on the sides of buildings or in steeples or on top of columns at street corners. I've been to towns in Maine and Tennessee, and once I went to Des Moines, Iowa, to fix a clock in a bank tower. Nowadays banks aren't built to look like banks. They are built to look like bungalows with drive-through carports. Nobody puts a clock on a bungalow."

Alex added, "My brother can repair chimes—a lost art." He studied Jake for a minute. "It's probably hard for a young man like yourself to believe that people once relied on the face of a public clock to tell them the time of day. And before clocks, there were mill whistles and church chimes. Time was measured in sections: mornings, afternoons, and nights. It wasn't too many years ago that measuring time by the quarter hour was accurate enough for most things, and the minute hand was good for boiling eggs."

"The second hand was invented as a form of persecution," Morris said.

Jacob laughed. "What do you have to say about nanoseconds?"

"Useless! You can't even say *nanosecond* in a nanosecond. Can a horse win a race by a nose and a nanosecond?" Jake shook his head. "In a nanosecond, can I even tell our little Margaret Rose that we are glad she is back here with us?" He reached over and patted my hand.

"How did you find the time to do the towers?" Jake asked.

"By not being in a hurry," Alex said. "That's how you find the time."

Uncle Morris pushed his chair back from the table and got up. He went to the kitchen counter to start the coffee. He ground the beans and set them into a filter and poured boiling water over them. Like the ancient Japanese tea ceremony, no part of the ritual was to be rushed. As we waited, I got up from the table to clear the dinner dishes. Jake got up too. "My job," I said. "You must sit still while they do coffee and dessert, or my uncles will think you're in a hurry. My uncles do not believe in hurrying any part of dinner."

As he was setting out the cups and saucers, Uncle Morris said, "Alex, my brother, he never asked me what I was doing. Never a question. What he was doing, what I was doing, we never discussed."

"Even when we dug the foundation for the first tower," Alex said, "even after we sank the first pilings, we never discussed it."

Morris said, "During World War II, we couldn't build much because the country needed all the scrap metal for the war effort. Then one day Alex started making pendants. The first ones were from the broken china and crystal that we had in our store. As it was with the towers, so it was with the pendants, also. My brother pointed to a spot. I knew what to do. Without discussion, I knew what he wanted. I drilled a hole, and we hung a pendant."

Alex said, "No rehearsals."

"After he used up the broken pieces we had from

the shop, he started buying glass and bottles from flea markets."

"Noxzema used to come in a pretty blue-glass jar," Alex said. "Also Phillips' Milk of Magnesia. They use blue plastic now. But most of the cobalt blue glass you see there is from those old jars. I like to mix the colors and also to mix glass and porcelain and the metal parts from Morris's old clocks."

"I saved all the old parts," Morris said. "Worn-out gears, I saved, and balance wheels. Sometimes there were chimes."

"There is a part inside a clock that is called an *escape wheel*. It is round and has sawteeth. I loved when Morris had one of those. Those I made into a feature attraction."

"And you didn't love when I brought home a balance spring?"

"Of course I loved the balance springs." He turned to Jake and pleaded, "Did you hear me say I didn't love the balance springs?"

Jake didn't know if he was to answer or not. Instead, he said, "The mix is good. I like it a lot."

Morris grunted. "The balance wheels, he bound with wire, and these he hung on the towers like earrings."

Alex nodded. "Yes, like earrings."

"Did you hang them so that some of them would strike one another like wind chimes?"

Alex got a faraway look in his eyes. "They sing, you know. When the wind blows, the towers sing. The wind decides the pitch. When it blows strong, the heavy ones sing bass and compete with the crystal, which is a soprano." He smiled to himself.

"Was that deliberate or a happy accident?" Jake asked.

Alex shrugged his Old World shrug. "The answer is yes and no. It just happened; it was worked out; it was an accident; it was planned. Maybe an accident led to a plan. Maybe the accident was part of a greater plan. Who knows?"

Uncle Morris said, "The Noxzema looks pretty, but it makes a clunky sound. To the Noxzema and the Milk of Magnesia, you shouldn't listen."

—Downtown was booming

After the war, the veterans returned, and college enrollment swelled, and so did the population. Margaret Rose Landau gave birth to my mother, Naomi. Mrs. Bevilaqua gave birth to Loretta, and Mrs. Vanderwaal had Peter.

Returning World War II veterans were getting married, and Jewels Bi-Rose was selling a lot of engagement rings and bridal shower gifts and strings of pearls for the groom to give to the bride and watches for the bride to give to the groom.

• • •

"After the war Morris started again making trips to repair town clocks. Those were the years when we could count on our sister, Margaret, to help out in the store. Our sister couldn't repair watches—only Morris could do that—but Margaret knew quality, and she knew how to be nice to customers. We could always count on her."

Morris said, "When our sister was living, we didn't need any Helgas or tattooed boys."

I said, "There was a girl in my cabin at camp who had a tattoo."

Uncle Morris was shocked. "A girl your age?" I nodded. "A real tattoo?" I nodded. Looking pained, Uncle Morris said to Jake, "Until these last few years, I didn't even know anyone with a tattoo except survivors from the concentration camps. And I can tell you, those tattoos were not a decoration. They were numbers. Numbers for purposes of identification. The Nazis turned people into numbers." He shook his head sadly. "But today, these kids decorate their arms and who knows what else. . . ." He looked over at me.

"Her *tush*," I said. "Ashley Schwartz has a tattoo on her tush."

Uncle Alex grinned. "A tattoo of what?" he asked.

"A rose," Jake answered.

"You've seen it?" I asked, shocked.

Jake smiled. "Of course I've seen it. Every time she puts on her bikini. If she didn't want people to see it, she would have had it below the bikini line." Uncle Morris was still shaking his head. Jake cleared his throat and changed the subject. "Where did the clock faces come from?"

Uncle Alex explained, "They were rescued. Rescued from the big clocks that were being demolished from urban renewal. When we got into the 1970s, urban renewal became the big thing. There had been riots in the big inner cities, and the government was trying to clean them up. What they did was demolish whole blocks of old buildings. Marble came down. Bricks fell. Everything old came down. High-rise glass buildings went up. And parking garages. Parking garages so that people would have a place for their cars when they drive to their offices from the suburbs. They don't stay downtown any longer than they have to. They do their business and then get back in their cars and go back to the suburbs."

Morris added, "They don't put big, fancy clocks on high-rise glass. I took all the clocks that no one wanted. The faces, we put on top of the towers. They came from all over. Different clocks all over. None of them match."

Alex laughed. "They don't match, but then, they don't tell time, either."

Jake said, "The way they're set, there's no way you can see two of them at once."

Uncle Alex said, "Not a lot of people figure that out." Now it was his turn to get up and announce, "Dessert will be Margaret's favorite."

We watched as he whipped cream with a wire whisk and set that bowl in the refrigerator. He removed a roll of chestnut pâté from the refrigerator, dipped a knife into warm water before cutting four slices from it, carefully placed each slice into a stemmed glass, replaced the rest of the pâté in the refrigerator, took a container of vanilla ice cream from the freezer, and slowly dished a double scoop into the glasses, drizzled chocolate sauce over the ice cream, and followed that with a huge dollop of whipped cream. Before he set my portion in front of me, he struck the side of the glass with a spoon to make it ring, then he lifted the glass and held it high and said, "Welcome home, *édes* Margitkám."

"Who is *édes* Margitkám?" Jake asked.

"I am."

"She's *my sweet Margaret*," Uncle Alex said.

"Mine too," Uncle Morris said.

Jake looked at me and said, "I wasn't so sure about that twenty-four hours ago, but I am now."

My favorite dessert deserved to be eaten slowly. The best way to slow down is to lick your spoon clean each time and to carefully apportion the whipped cream, the ice cream, and the chestnut pâté carefully so that all three flavors finish together. Spoon licking and apportioning make you savor each mouthful.

Uncle Morris poured the coffee.

Jake took a sip and said, "I could swoon. The only thing that would make this the tiniest bit better would be if you wouldn't mind my smoking a cigar."

"Go right ahead."

Jake reached into the bib pocket of his coveralls and took out two fresh cigars. "Will you join me?"

Uncle Morris did. Uncle Alex did not.

After two very long puffs, Jake asked, "Why did you paint them? Was that to protect them?"

Uncle Alex shrugged his Old World shrug. "They were not rusting. They are stainless steel, and the wires are copper."

"Maybe you just needed to take things to the next level," Jake suggested.

"I don't know from levels," Uncle Morris said. "What my brother needed was exaggeration."

"Maybe it was time for rock 'n' roll," Jake said.

Uncle Alex smiled. "Maybe," he said. "Maybe that's the way to put it. But it was also true that business was slowing down and down. There was more time. Much more time." Uncle added, "The first time we ran out of paint, we tried to make a match, but we couldn't. The new paint never matched the old. We never could judge how much we needed and were always running out of one color or another. So when we ran out of the original color, we would just mix something new. By the time summer was over, the sun would fade the brightest shades, so the colors never blended altogether."

"Very interesting," Jake said. "That accounts for the camouflage pattern."

"You don't like it?" Uncle Morris asked.

"Oh, I do. I do like it. I like it a lot. I didn't mean to say that I don't like it."

"People don't say *interesting* when they really like something," Morris said. "*Interesting* is what people say when they don't like something but don't want to say they don't."

"I was trying to say that *how it happened* was interesting."

I said to Jake, "Do you want me to tell you how it happened last spring?" He nodded. "Last spring my uncles let me mix up a batch of paint, so I added some of this and some of that and ended up with a pale orange color that looked like peach in dim light and apricot when the light was bright. There was no color like it anywhere on the towers."

"It was extraordinary," Uncle Alex said. "Like an orange sherbet."

Uncle Morris added, "It was unique. Not *interesting*. It was decorative. Very nice. *Very* nice."

"There was some paint left over, so we used Margitkám's orange sherbet for maintenance all of last summer," Uncle Alex said.

"This year I was supposed to make lemon and lime to go with it," I said, "but I got sent off to camp." It occurred to me just then that I would be able to help paint while I was there. "I can mix up the lemon and lime now," I said. "We'll have our fruit cocktail after all."

"We'll see, Margitkám," Uncle Alex said. But he did not look at me when he said it. "It's very artistic already."

"Leave it," Morris said severely to his brother. Then, softening his tone, he said to me, "It's very artistic even without the lemon and lime, *édes* Margitkám. Very artistic."

—business was slowing down and down
In 1965 the Fivemile Creek Mall, a vast regional mall, heated in winter and air-conditioned in summer, opened. It was located near the county line, far from downtown, but it had parking spaces for a thousand cars.

Osmond's Department Store moved out of downtown and into the mall. Halley's Hardware became part of the Ace Hardware chain and moved into a strip mall on the state road. The drugstore became a Walgreens and followed the exodus. The Tivoli, an old-fashioned movie theater with chandeliers and a stage and a balcony, tried to hold on by becoming a second-run, dollar movie house, but it had to close.

After office hours, the streets of downtown were deserted.

People couldn't wait to move out of the neighborhood. The Vanderwaals left, and so did the Bevilaquas. Those who could not sell their houses rented them, most often to students from Clarion College who were grateful for the cheap rent.

Jake asked, "What happened to Jewels Bi-Rose?"

"We lost it," Morris said abruptly.

Uncle Alex explained, "Shoppers had all moved to the suburbs. They had to come to us by car. Parking was tight. People couldn't be sure they would have a place for their car like at the mall. Jewels Bi-Rose was not doing enough business to pay the rent."

"We held out until 1970, the year our sister died."

"Then we closed."

—we closed

When Clarion State College became Clarion State University, the school built more dormitories as well as apartments for married students—even a day-care center for students with children. Soon the houses around Schuyler Place went empty. They had received more high spirits than high maintenance from the college crowd, so by the time they went on the rental market again, they were in bad shape. The neighborhood went from unkempt to undesirable. During the day, the streets were empty of people and filled with litter. The Bevilaquas' house was the first to be boarded up. At night vagrants lifted the boards from the windows and took shelter in the empty rooms.

Morris and Alex took down the mailbox and had a slot cut into their front door. If a package was to be delivered, the mail-man left a yellow notification card, and Morris went to the post office to pick it up.

No one came into the neighborhood unless they had to.

"But you stayed here," Jake said. "I know the towers must have—"

Uncle Morris interrupted. "The truth? After we paid off our debts, we couldn't afford to move."

"After we closed the store, we set up a little business here at the house. We used the dining room. Morris had his watch repair shop near the front window. I did a little business in antique china, glass, and silver. All my merchandise fit in one display case. I also did special orders for people who couldn't find a particular pattern. We put a little *Jewels Bi-Rose* sign out front."

"A mistake," Morris added. "It was not an advertisement. It was an invitation."

"We were robbed three times—no, four . . ."

"That's four times within a year and a half. Every six months . . ."

". . . like clockwork," Uncle Alex finished, and the brothers looked at each other and started to laugh.

Jake looked puzzled at first, but then he, too, started to laugh.

Still laughing, Uncle Alex said, "We got to be professional victims. The first time we were robbed, people lost their heirloom watches that they had brought in for repair. After that, we hid the good stuff and kept the safe full of junk. Some money—just so they could go away with ready cash. But mostly junk." Alex wiped tears from his eyes and asked his brother, "Do you remember the time that crook dropped that Daum crystal bowl?"

"Remember? Of course I remember." Morris looked at Jake and said, "It was a beautiful piece. Amber glass. An antique. I asked the crook to save us the pieces. So he picked them up and cut his hand. He got furious. He hit me on the head. Knocked me out."

Uncle Alex continued, "After that, we kept handcuffs and socks and tape handy. We found that if we were tied up, the crooks felt safe and wouldn't beat us up. We didn't want them getting nervous. A nervous crook is a dangerous crook."

"The clean socks were so that they wouldn't gag us with a filthy rag. We got so that we could tell the combination to the safe with a gag in our mouths." The brothers looked at each other and broke out laughing again.

Jake asked, "Did they ever catch any of the thieves?"

"Yeah. Those kids who broke the Daum crystal bowl. They left bloody fingerprints, and they had a record."

"What happened to them?"

Alex answered, "They got a few months in jail, but we didn't get any of our merchandise back. Then while Morris and I were at the courthouse testifying—" He started to giggle, and Uncle Morris caught it. As soon as one of them slowed down, the other lobbed it right back. Jake and I watched, as if at a tennis match, and soon we were laughing, too, even though we did not know why we were, except that we couldn't not. Finally, between gasps, Uncle Alex said, "While we were at the courthouse testifying, we were robbed again."

And Uncle Morris caught his breath long enough to add, "Why should they miss an opportunity like that?"

Uncle Alex said, "The police let us collect the pieces

after they were finished with them. I'll show you the Daum crystal pendants if you like." He smiled and added, "They are the only parts of the towers that are recorded history."

Morris said, "This is the strangest thing: Even after the neighborhood got dangerous and we were being robbed on a regular basis, no one hurt the towers. Isn't that funny?"

"I would call it a tribute," Jake said. "Even Leonardo da Vinci didn't escape vandalism. His model of the horse for the duke of Milan was used for target practice by the French soldiers who conquered Milan." Jake looked out the kitchen window. It was too dark for him to see anything, but he said anyway, "This looks like a nice neighborhood now. I noticed that the houses on either side of you are freshly painted. The yards look nice, and so do the sidewalks. Everything looks to be in good repair."

"Not repaired," Morris corrected. "Don't say *repaired*. Say *restored*." He put his forefinger to his lips and said, "And don't call it *urban renewal*. Our town fathers made that perfectly clear. Urban renewal would mean that they would tear down all the old run-down buildings and build new ones—bigger and higher. Now they say they are preserving the past. They call it *redevelopment*."

Uncle Alex explained, "Our neighborhood has been officially designated as historical and *charming.*"

Uncle Morris said, "I spit on charming."

Uncle Alex said, "The Rose brothers used to live in a neighborhood. Now we live in Old Town."

—call it redevelopment

After the neighborhood around Schuyler Place went from bad to blighted, the city leaders created the Historic Downtown Trust Fund. This was a large sum of government money put aside to loan to people who wanted to buy any of the derelict downtown buildings and restore them. The Uncles' neighborhood qualified.

The city bought the old Osmond's Department Store building and converted it into government offices. They closed off Summit Street downtown and made it into a pedestrian mall.

Being close to City Hall and the county offices, Old Town was a good place for young professionals, especially lawyers, to set up offices. The houses were cheap, and using the trust fund money, they got low-interest loans to convert them into offices with all the necessities of modern electrical wiring and plumbing. All they had to do was agree to obey the regulations about preserving the historical integrity of Old Town. They could restore but not change the front of their houses, and they were to use approved colors when they painted. As part of the restoration project, trust fund money was also used to pave the alleys and stripe them for parking.

"We got a small business loan from the bank and opened the Time Zone—a kiosk on the ground floor of the Fivemile Creek Mall."

Morris said, "Most modern watches and clocks need batteries, not a repairman. Nothing ticks anymore. People don't like ticking. Humming is acceptable, but no ticktock. People love digital. With digital, kids don't even have to learn how to tell time." He made a face. "I spit on digital."

Alex explained, "We sell watchbands and batteries and what are called fun watches to pay the rent. And *occhiali antisole.*"

"Oh, yes. Must not forget the sunglasses," Uncle Morris said. Even the ends of his mustache turned down. "Here in Old Town, in the pedestrian mall, where Jewels Bi-Rose used to be, the stores that once sold goods and services now sell tchotchkes and three-dollar cups of coffee with as many varieties as Heinz has ketchup."

Uncle Alex said, "Heinz has only one variety of ketchup."

"It has fifty-seven. Every bottle of ketchup says 'Heinz 57 Varieties.'"

"That's what it is, fifty-seven varieties."

"And isn't Heinz ketchup?"

"Of course Heinz is ketchup. All the world knows that Heinz means ketchup."

"And does it also mean fifty-seven varieties?"

"Of course. It's their trademark. But either you have Heinz ketchup *or* you have fifty-six other Heinz varieties."

"If that's what you insist."

"I insist."

"May I continue?" Uncle Morris asked.

Uncle Alex nodded and muttered, "One ketchup. Only one."

Uncle Morris glared at him and said, "I'm continuing, with your permission." Uncle Alex glared back before Uncle Morris continued. "Where Jewels Bi-Rose was is now Tees for Two. Buy one, get the second one for two dollars more. They are selling T-shirts that say things that even the ACLU would want to flush down the toilet."

Jake looked at me and laughed. "I've had experience with T-shirts that have been flushed down the toilet—or shower."

Uncle Morris said, "You can get fifty-seven varieties"—with a sideways glance at Alex—"of cappuccino"—he paused for emphasis—"or patchouli and every other form of incense and nonsense, but there is not a single place to buy a box of detergent or a roll of toilet paper in the new old downtown."

—officially charming

Hapgood, Hapgood, and Martin, the oldest and most prestigious law firm in Epiphany, converted 21 Schuyler Place into offices for their young associates. The city was proud to have them. After they moved in, the business section of the Epiphany Times ran a banner headline that said LAW FIRM STAKES ITS FUTURE ON THE PAST. *The article featured a four-column-wide, four-inch-long picture showing Taylor Hapgood holding a piece of paper. The caption under the picture explained that he was holding the original deed to the Vanderwaal house. The article quoted Taylor Hapgood, the senior partner in the firm, as saying that he had invested more money in fiber-optic wiring than the original cost of the house had been when the Vanderwaals had purchased it from the Tappan Glass Works.*

Geoffrey and Gwendolyn Klinger, both lawyers, moved into 17 Schuyler Place, the house where the Bevilaquas once lived.

"But your property is valuable again," Jake said. Morris and Alex exchanged a look, and Jake asked, "Isn't it?"

"Yeah, sure," Uncle Morris said. "Valuable."

Uncle Alex massaged his neck and leaned his head

back. He closed his eyes and said, "We have lawyers on our right and lawyers on our left. And if lawyers know anything, they know property values." He charged forward, opened his eyes, and grimaced. "And how to protect them."

eleven

I told the Uncles that Jake wanted to paint a rose ceiling for me. "A giant rose rose from wall to wall on my ceiling."

Uncle Morris said, "Very nice. Very decorative."

Uncle Alex said, "Very nice." Then, looking mischievously at Jake, he added, "Very *interesting.*"

"When? When will he do this thing?"

"On Wednesdays," Jake answered. "Wednesday is my day off. I'll start the day after tomorrow, if that's not too soon."

"He'll need a scaffold, Uncles," I said.

"That is no problem. No problem whatsoever."

"Not at all," Uncle Morris said.

"I'll bring the paint," Jake said. "I have many shades of rose, but first I'll need to see the room to measure the ceiling."

The energetic, cheerful Jacob Kaplan who took the stairs two at a time was hardly the shuffling handyman who had fixed the shower in Meadowlark cabin. This man walked around humming under his breath. This man smiled as he took the measurements of the room and studied the ceiling. "It's almost square," he said. "I'll need to draw a grid. Do you think one of your uncles will help?"

"I know Uncle Alex will be happy to help," I replied. There was no question in my mind that he would. My father complained that the Uncles spoiled me. It was true that they did let me have whatever I wanted, but I had always figured that that was because I never asked for anything they didn't want to give me. It was equally true that they let me do whatever I wanted, but that, too, was only because I never asked to be allowed to do anything that they didn't want to allow. "Uncle Alex takes the afternoon shift at the Time Zone, so he'll be available in the morning."

Jake sat on the edge of my bed. "And you, Miss Margaret Rose, I'll need you to go to the library and find a picture of the most beautiful rose rose you can find. You better love it, because it will be very large and it will be with you forever."

"I'll do it tomorrow."

Jake said, "Good!" and he looked up at the ceiling again.

I hesitated to ask, but I had to. "Are you being so nice to me because your mother wasn't?"

Jake's eyes stayed focused on the ceiling, and when

he did look at me, he asked me to stand in front of him so that we could be eye to eye. "That's part of the reason."

I was secretly hoping that it would not be any part of the reason.

"And there is something else."

"What else?"

"I admired your resistance and your uncle's determination to rescue you." Standing there, eye to eye as he sat on the edge of the bed, he took both of my hands in his. "Margaret, you have to understand that my mother is ill equipped to handle girls who have a vocabulary that matches hers. And she is no match at all for your uncle. He is like a stealth bomber. You can't see what's coming until you've been wiped out. I like him a lot. Morris, too." He let my hands go and looked out the window. It was too dark to see the towers, but I knew he was picturing them in his mind's eye.

My voice barely above a whisper, I asked, "You fell in love, didn't you?" And then, embarrassed at mentioning the word *love* to a person of the opposite sex, particularly to this person of the opposite sex, I quickly added, "You fell in love with the towers, didn't you?"

"I guess it's love, but it is something more. It's a longing to be in love."

Relieved that Jake had not misinterpreted my

remark about love, yet disappointed that he had not, I said, "Like *why not* paint a rose ceiling?"

"Exactly," he said. "There is no reason to paint a rose ceiling, and there is no reason not to. It is *areasonable,* isn't it, Margaret?" Too dry-mouthed to answer, I nodded. "I've longed to do something areasonable for a very long time. The towers made me realize how much. I don't mind fixing toilets and cleaning out showers, and I don't even mind being the camp idiot—actually, I am the camp idiot by choice—and I know that painting billboards is not art; it's hardly a craft, but I loved doing it. I loved it because it was doing something big, the way your uncles love doing the towers. Sometimes I wonder about that need in me. I go to these craft fairs in the mall, and I see all these wooden puzzles and birdhouses and patchwork place mats and painted tin buckets, and I know that there are a lot of people like me who have a need to make things. It's like asking why we speak. We speak because we are human and because we can. Your uncles build towers because they are men and because they can. I understand the towers. They speak to me. Their language is exotic, but their alphabet is familiar. I understand what they are saying. I do. I really do."

"What do you think they are saying?"

"They are telling me a story. A story full of sense and nonsense. They are saying that if life has a structure, a staff, a sensible scaffold, we hang our nonsense on it. And they are saying that broken parts add color and music to the staff of life. And they also say that when you know that your framework has been built right and strong, it's all right to add color to it, too. The towers are saying, there is no *why*—only a *why-not*. That's what the towers say to me." He reached out and took my hands between his, pressing them together like cymbals. "So I say to you, my sweet Margaret, *why not* paint a rose ceiling? Besides, it gives me a wonderful place to come to on my day off."

All the way down the sixteen steps from the second floor to the first, I could feel the touch of his hands where he had held mine when he called me *my sweet Margaret*.

Uncle Alex was feeding Tartufo, and Uncle Morris was washing the supper dishes. I picked up a dishtowel and started drying dishes, not totally aware that I was doing so. Uncle Morris pointed to the wall phone and asked Jake if he would like to call his mother.

"I prefer not to," he said. He winked at me. The second time he ever did. "But I will. I'll call her from a pay phone on my way home."

He left. The Uncles finished putting away the dishes and silverware, and I gathered up the soiled napkins to put in the upstairs hamper.

I kissed my uncles good night and climbed the stairs with something in my heart that had never been there before.

Perfidy in Epiphany

twelve

I awakened to the smell of pancakes. I knew they wouldn't be ordinary pancakes. They would be *palacsinta,* the thin crepes made with flour, milk, eggs, and carbonated water that Uncle fried one at a time, spread with jam, and rolled.

I rushed downstairs in my pajamas.

I would have three to start.

Dressed, ready for the Time Zone, Uncle Morris was sitting at the table reading the morning paper and drinking coffee. The minute he saw me, he quickly folded the paper and stashed it on the seat of the chair on his left.

"Good morning," he said. He had always before greeted me with *Jó reggelt,* which is *good morning* in Hungarian, then he would wait for me to repeat the Hungarian. Uncle Alex would add his *Jó reggelt,* and I would repeat it for him, too.

This morning, Uncle Alex said nothing—did not even greet me in English—but stood at the stove, with his back to me, pouring batter into a pan. He tipped and twisted the pan until the small amount of batter covered its surface. When the top of the batter bubbled, he flipped the pancake and allowed it to fry for only four or five seconds more before turning it out onto a plate.

Even Tartufo did not give me his usual greeting. He sat at Uncle's legs, greedily watching every movement of batter and batter-maker. Only after I was seated did he get up and make his way over to me. I petted him and told him, "Good dog," and when his tail started thumping the floor with pleasure, I whispered that he could have one of my *palacsinta*.

Without turning around, Uncle Alex said, "But no jelly. Gives him bad breath." He spread plum jelly on three of the *palacsinta,* rolled them up, sprinkled them with powdered sugar, and set them on a plate in front of me. Then he sat down across from me, waited until I had taken my first bite, and asked, "Good?"

"Very."

Uncle Morris got up. *"Jaj, Istenem!"* he exclaimed. "It's late. I better get going."

The early shift at the Time Zone went from ten to six; the late shift, from one to nine. I looked at the kitchen clock. It was only a quarter to nine. He never left the house before a quarter after. Uncle Morris was always "running late." In his role as Father Time, my dad would complain, "Morris Rose is a watchmaker, and the man has absolutely no sense of time." And every time my mother "ran late" he maintained that she had learned it from him.

Uncle Morris took his jacket from the back of his chair. "Will you be okay while Alex and I are both gone, Margitkám?" he asked.

I told him that I had a busy day ahead. I had to unpack my camp gear, wash my clothes and my hair, and that would take up practically the whole morning. "I also have to go to the library to choose a picture of a rose rose, and I know that will take a very long time because I need to find the perfect one." I reminded them that they had promised to put up a scaffold. "Jake said that he'll be here on Wednesday. That's tomorrow."

"But there is the night, Margitkám," Uncle Alex said. "We're used to working at night."

"The pipe is ready. Alex will bring it up from the basement. All we have to do is fit the pieces together. The scaffold will be waiting for him."

Uncle Morris leaned over and kissed the top of my head. I looked up, told him good-bye, took another bite of *palacsinta,* and closed my eyes, trying to shut out all sensations except taste. When I opened my eyes, Uncle Morris was standing by the door exchanging a look with Uncle Alex and shaking his head no. "Don't forget your paper," Uncle Alex said. He grabbed it, nervously folded it over three times, and shoved it—really shoved it—under Uncle Morris's arm.

Pressing the paper close to his ribs, Uncle Morris stiffly opened the screen door. "Well, I'm off," he said, and didn't move. He and Uncle Alex exchanged another look. That puzzled me.

"Go already!" Uncle Alex said. Uncle Morris didn't budge. Uncle Alex turned away from the stove and waved his spatula in the air. "Go, Morris! Go to work." I watched the screen door close. Uncle Alex turned back to the stove, flushed. The *palascinta* had burned. He mumbled under his breath and threw the ruined pancake in the trash. He turned to me and said, "He made me scorch the pan. I'll have to start with a clean one now."

I put my fork down, feeling uneasy.

"Would you care for another?"

"I guess so," I said.

"What? You only guess so? If you don't want more, just say so. I won't bother scrubbing the pan. . . ."

"I would like two more, Uncle."

"Only two?"

"No. Three. I forgot the one for Tartufo."

After breakfast, I went upstairs and gathered up my camp clothes and took them to the basement. On my way to the washer, I passed my uncles' workshop. I dumped everything into the washer. Everything, whether I had worn it or not. Half listening to the sound of the washing machine fill with water, I entered the workshop and looked around. A layer of dust had settled everywhere. The Uncles had never been very good at keeping order, but this was not disorder as much as it was neglect. I ran my finger through the thick dust on the worktable where Uncle Alex made his pendants. In the far corner of the room there were three sacks of Portland cement. They were for the base of Tower Four. They, too, were covered with dust.

The washer had finished filling up. There was a click, and the *slosh-squish, slosh-squish* of the wash cycle began a low rhythmic undertone to the discordant sounds I had heard at breakfast. There had been no cheerful *Jó reggelt.* There had been: *You only guess so? If you don't want more, just say so.* Uncle Alex had never before been that irritable with me. Being irritable with his brother was normal, but never with me. Never. If there was one thing my uncles agreed with each other about, it was how wonderful I was. My uncles had never before exchanged glances with each other over me.

I lifted the lid of the washer and saw that everything was being agitated. Good. The soil of Talequa would soon go down the drain.

I went upstairs and passed through the far side of the kitchen. Uncle Alex was again standing at the stove. He glanced over at me briefly and let me go out the back door without a comment or a smile.

—without the lemon and lime

I wandered over to the far side of Tower Two. I lifted a chip of paint with my fingernail and watched as it fluttered to the ground. I stood inside the tower ribs and looked up. The paint was flaking all over.

This past spring, Morris had planted his peppers and Alex had tended his roses, but instead of starting maintenance on the towers, Uncle Alex had announced that they were taking Tartufo to Texas.

I had asked why, and Uncle Alex had said that there was a report that the filbert trees in a large orchard had developed barren circles around their bases. Such circles, called *burn patterns,* are a sign of truffles. I had asked why Uncle Morris was also going.

Uncle Alex had replied, "He's never been to Texas."

"But he hates Tartufo."

"Truffles can bring in eight hundred dollars a pound. Even my brother finds that acceptable."

I had asked if they would be back in time to take care of me while my mother and father were in Peru. "I'll mix up the lemon and lime paint to go with the orange sherbet."

And that was when Uncle Alex had suggested that camp might be good for me. He said that because I was an only child, a group experience might be a good thing. I was shocked. I told him that like every other only child on the planet, I was no more responsible for being *only* than I was for being a child. My own mother, Naomi, whom he loved as much as he loved me, had been an only child and had never had a camp experience, and everyone—with the possible exception of my father—thought that she had turned out perfect. Besides, if he had gone to school in this country instead of in the Old World, he would know that grades K through six give a person enough group experience to last the rest of her life.

I had just gotten over the shock of discovering that my parents had no intention of taking me with them, and now I had to face the fact that my uncles didn't want me either. I could not understand why no one wanted to solve the "What to do with Margaret" problem. I could not understand why they even saw it as a problem.

I avoided my uncles after that, and I avoided my parents, too, except for the goods and services required by me, a minor who could not yet drive a car or earn a living wage. I spoke when spoken to and directed all my attention to my hurt feelings and the mountain of camp brochures I had sent for.

When the Uncles returned from Texas, Uncle Morris called. I knew that his calling me was quite a concession, for Uncle Morris was convinced that telephones rotted the ears and were responsible for his hearing loss. He almost never made a phone call voluntarily. He told me that he and Uncle Alex had brought me a present from Texas. Summoning up all the indifference I could command, I managed not to ask what it was or when I could get it. This resulted in a long telephone pause that began to rot my ears. So to end the ear-rotting silence, I asked if Tartufo had found a truffle. He had not.

I moved back out from under the cage of tower ribs and poked my finger into a paint blister. I watched it deflate, leaving a wrinkled skin of mauve like an untreated wound. The dust in the workshop, the blisters and flakes of paint were sending me a message. Something was wrong.

I returned to the kitchen. Uncle Alex had the refrigerator door open and was studying its contents. Tartufo pranced between me and Uncle, his feet making ticktock noises on the linoleum floor. Still keeping his back to me, Uncle Alex continued to look inside the refrigerator. "I know I have some cottage cheese."

"You have your hand right on it, Uncle."

"Oh, yes, so I do."

I said, "Put it down, Uncle. Please."

Uncle Alex closed the refrigerator door and sat down opposite me. Tartufo calmed down and sat by Uncle's chair. Uncle concentrated on petting Tartufo. He would not look me in the eye. "I'm thinking of having Tartufo groomed," he said. "It might improve his looks. People are so impressed by appearances. They don't realize what a valuable dog Tartufo is. Do you realize that truffles sell for eight hundred dollars a pound? Eight hundred dollars."

Uncle Alex was chattering away like a talk-show host, looking at Tartufo as if he were a cue card for a subject to use up time. I never knew either of the Uncles to care about money. "Uncle!" I said. "I think you ought to tell me what's going on. You'll be using the pipe for the fourth tower for the scaffold, won't you?"

"Why not? We have it. It's ready."

"There isn't going to be a fourth tower, is there, Uncle?"

"You want a one-word answer?" I nodded. "No. A two-word answer would be: Definitely no."

"Why?"

"Would be a waste of time."

"That never bothered you before."

"When you get older, *édes* Margitkám, you'll realize

that all you have is time. You have time and your side of history. And that's all you have." He slapped his hands on his thighs and stood up. "Blintzes," he said. "I'll fry up the extra *palacsinta* batter and fill them with cottage cheese. We'll have blintzes for lunch tomorrow. Do you think Jake will like that?"

Of course he would, I thought, but I couldn't answer. I was aching with uneasiness. Something was wrong. It was in the kitchen and in the Tower Garden. It was in the air. All of 19 Schuyler Place was uneasy, but I didn't know why. Uncle asked me again if I thought Jake would like blintzes. He didn't even look at me to see me nod yes. He just went about scooping the cottage cheese out of the carton.

thirteen

At the library I went first to the art section. I found a rose rose in *The Roses*, by Pierre-Joseph Redouté. It should have been perfect. It should have been the rose I wanted. It was artistic, and I wanted Jake to think I liked artistic. It was historical, and I wanted Jake to think I liked historical. It was scientific, and it was pretty, but it was not passionate. I looked in other art books, but none of the painted roses had the moist, fleshy look of a single one of the roses on my uncle's bushes. So against my very own wishes, I went to the gardening section.

There, in the first book I pulled from the shelf, was the rose rose I wanted. It was multiple shades of passionate rose. Many multiple shades. It looked as if touching the page would stain your fingers. Even though it was a photograph and not a painting, even though it was not historical, even though it was not the rose that should be right, even though it came from the gardening section and not the art section, it was exactly the rose I wanted on my ceiling.

As I waited at the checkout counter, two copies of the *Epiphany Times* were on a horizontal rack nearby. One copy had the metro section facing out, and I was drawn to it, but I heard "Next," so I stepped up, had my book stamped, and left the library excited about the ceiling project and the thought of Jake's return visit.

I entered 19 Schuyler Place through the Tower Garden, as I usually did. Uncle Alex had left for work by the time I got back. I walked through the kitchen and through the front hall on my way upstairs. I laid the book of roses on the front hall table and picked up a numbered list that Uncle Alex had left:

1. *Took your clothes out of the washer*
2. *Put them in the dryer*
3. *Weren't dry yet when I left*
4. *Help yourself to anything in the refrigerator*
5. *Please walk Tartufo*
6. *Anytime this afternoon will be fine*
7. *Be careful crossing the streets*
8. *Glad you're here*

I studied his Old World handwriting. His 1s had little flags and his 7s had crosses. I read number 8 twice.

I found Tartufo's leash and headed outside. The mail had been delivered and was lying on the floor just inside the front door. I picked the letters up—mostly envelopes with little windows—but there was a postcard with a picture of the Andes. It was from my mother.

> *Dear Uncles,*
>
> *The dig is going well. It seems strange that we are here cherishing the smallest shard of an ancient city when Epiphany is about to tear down the best monuments it ever had. I guess the towers are not ancient enough. Keep your spirits up. Have you heard from Margaret?*
>
>
>
> *Love,*
>
> *Naomi*
>

I couldn't believe what I read the first time, so I read the card two times more:

Epiphany is about to tear down the best monuments it ever had.

The towers! The towers were coming down.

And there in the hall with only Tartufo to hear me, I howled. My roar filled the hall, climbed the stairs, and echoed back. Bubbles of rage swelled and burst inside the hollow that the Alums had scraped bare. I hugged my stomach and doubled over in agony. I collapsed on the bottom step. I tried to read the card again, but the words stung my eyes. I clutched the postcard to my chest and began to rock back and forth in a pulse as primitive as pain. With no one but Tartufo to bear witness, I began to moan. I rocked and moaned, motion and sound keeping time with the spasms of my aching heart. I gave voice to all the deep, sad sounds I had tamped into silence since summer began. I gave voice to the cries I had suppressed when the Rockette Alums had herded me up to my bunk. I gave vent to the answers I had crippled inside me when Mrs. Kaplan and I had had our little chats. I moaned and rocked and did not stop until Tartufo nuzzled his nose into the bend of my arms. He needed comfort, too. "The towers are coming down," I said. I could speak now, softly now, and I said it again. "The towers are coming down, Tartufo. Why didn't I guess?"

Grokking sounds came from deep inside Tartufo. I took him off the leash and said, "You have to stay here, Tartufo. I've got to go back to the library." I lightly touched his back, and he understood. He sat, statue-like; without my even having to say *Stay,* he stayed. I slipped the postcard into the book of roses and stacked the rest of the mail on the hall table, and I was out the door.

There on page one of the Metro News section of the *Epiphany Times* was the headline:

DEMOLITION SCHEDULED

The three-year battle to save the clock towers on Schuyler Place will come to an end in ten days. The city has awarded the contract to demolish the structures to Foscaro Brothers of Albany.

Concern about the safety of the structures initiated a petition by the Home Owners Association of Old Town to have them taken down. They were built without permits. The city grants permits only after approval of building plans that guarantee safety. Morris Rose and his brother, Alexander, built the towers over a period of the last forty-five years without plans.

The Home Owners Association of Old Town is concerned that high winds could topple the towers and destroy property adjacent to the towers as well as several houses nearby. At a council hearing on April 4, Kenneth Hawkins, chief of the Building and Safety Department, said that because they were built without blueprints, there is no way to ascertain if the structures are safe. To avoid risk, Hawkins recommended that the towers be demolished.

Taylor Hapgood, one of the pioneers in the restoration of Old Town, praised the decision. "These structures simply do not fit the historical integrity of the neighborhood. They are unsafe, and they have become a blight on the neighborhood. They detract from the dignity of Old Town."

On behalf of the Home Owners Association, he has asked the city to defray the costs of the demolition as part of the Greater Comprehensive Redevelopment Plan, the city-funded initiative to restore downtown as well as the neighborhoods around Town Square.

The Rose brothers made their last appeal at the April 8 meeting of the city council. The council voted in favor of the Home Owners Association and posted for bids for the demolition. Foscaro Brothers estimate that removing the structures from such a high-density urban area will take three weeks. Money for the project will come from the Historic Downtown Trust Fund.

I put the paper back on the library rack, ran outside, and bought one from the coin box on the corner. I sat on a bench in Town Square and read the article three more times. Then I tucked the paper under my arm and crossed the street to City Hall.

I stopped at the reception desk in the front lobby, introduced myself, and, pointing to the article in the paper, asked for directions to the section of public records. "I need a record of the city council meeting for April eighth of this year."

The receptionist said, "We are afraid that for security reasons, we cannot allow you into the records room without a pass." I listened to her *we,* and I looked at her smile—a twin of Mrs. Kaplan's—and I knew that the desk between us was her shield, and the rules, her sword.

With a lot more assurance than I felt, I said, "I was taught that council proceedings are a matter of public record. I am a public, and I need to see that record."

She repeated, "For security reasons, we cannot allow anyone without a pass into the records room." Repetition often serves as reason among the desk-empowered.

I was not about to back down. "Then please get someone who has a pass who can get the record for me." I reinforced my excellent manners with another "Please." I sat down on one of the chairs that were set against the wall. "I am prepared to wait all day today, you know." I crossed my arms over my chest and added, "And all day tomorrow, if that's what it takes."

The receptionist said, "Let us see what we can do." She picked up the phone and, holding her hand over the speaker, asked, "What did you say your name was?" I gave her my names, all three of them—slowly, syllable by syllable—and nodded each time she repeated it into the phone.

Within a few minutes, a woman wearing a picture ID on a chain, which swung like a clock pendulum with every step, hurried toward me. She was only halfway across the lobby when she called out. "Margaret, Margaret Kane, how are you, dear?" I hardly had time to answer before the woman said, "I feel so bad. I've been meaning to tell Peter what is happening. I promised myself I would, and then, what with one thing and another, I just haven't. Just haven't. It's Mr. Vanderwaal and the dialysis, you know. I thank God for the medical profession and dialysis, but his condition is chronic, you know, and the dialysis, it's up to three times a week at this point." She paused for breath. "You're here about the towers, aren't you?"

I nodded.

"When I read today's paper, I knew I should have said something sooner. Peter loves those towers. He visits the old neighborhood every time he comes home. I know I should have told him, but ..." She looked at me expecting a nod of understanding, but I was sorting things out: *Vanderwaal.* This was Mrs. Vanderwaal. And the Peter she referred to, the Peter who loved the towers? He was my mother's childhood friend.

Mrs. Vanderwaal was saying, "... I didn't want to give Peter anything more to worry about. He has enough to worry him, you know. His job, his papa, and the dialysis."

I was bewildered. How could everyone know—*have known*—and not say anything? They had all known for months, *for years,* and no one—*no one*—not one single person, relative or stranger, had uttered a word to me. Not everyone had the dialysis excuse. It was a conspiracy of silence.

Mrs. Vanderwaal stopped excusing herself long enough to look at me. "You didn't know, did you, dear?"

I shook my head. "Not until today."

"Well now, you just come along with me." She put her arms around my shoulders and said to the receptionist, "Lillian, please give this young lady a temp pass."

My pass was a different color from Mrs. Vanderwaal's, and it didn't have my picture. The chain was so long that it got caught between my legs when I took my first step. I didn't say much. Didn't have to. Mrs. Vanderwaal talked as we mounted the flight of stairs and as she filled out a request slip to obtain the records for the council proceedings of April 8. "I'll get you a printout, dear," she said. "I know I should have sent Peter printouts of everything, and I hate myself for being so neglectful, but I'm just months away from retirement. Mr. Vanderwaal—he's already retired, you know—we were going to get a Winnebago and travel around the country, but then this dialysis thing, three times a week now, came up, so I guess our Winnebago dreams are over. They've asked me to stay on here, and I think I will. Beats sitting around the house all day waiting for Mr. Vanderwaal's dialysis three times a week." She put the pen down. "Now, if you'll excuse me, I'll take this over to Eric and get things started."

I waited in her cubicle. On her desk was a picture of my mother, Peter, and Loretta Bevilaqua standing in front of Tower Two. My mother and Loretta looked to be about my age; they had no breasts. They were mugging for the camera. Peter was sitting on top of the tower, which was not much taller than either of the girls, and he had a hand on the top of each of their heads.

Mrs. Vanderwaal returned, and before she could say *dialysis* one more time, I asked about Peter.

"Peter actually got into his line of work because of those towers."

"What work is that, Mrs. Vanderwaal?"

"Museum work. He went to Brown University. That's the Ivy League, you know."

I didn't know, but I nodded. "Where is he now?"

"He lives in Wisconsin. Town by the name of Sheboygan. He's director of an art center there."

"I would like to call him."

"Yes, you should. I'll give you his number," she said. "Such a shame about the towers. I should have called him about them long before this." She wrote a number down on a Post-it and handed it to me. "These Post-its are wonderful. I think they were invented in Wisconsin. No, maybe it was Michigan. I know it was somewhere out there in the Midwest, so even if it was Michigan, it would be close to Peter in Wisconsin."

I asked about Loretta Bevilaqua.

"I don't know too much about her since she's grown. I know she got married"—here Mrs. Vanderwaal leaned in close to me and whispered—"and divorced. I think she has some kind of big job in New York City. A real career woman. Right in Manhattan. I heard that in one month she pays so much rent that it would go for a whole year's taxes if she lived in

Epiphany. Her mother is still living here. Not in the old neighborhood, of course, but she's still local. Assisted living, you know. You can call her. She'll tell you how to get in touch."

A skinny young man with a health-food-style, vegetarian-skimpy beard approached holding a few long sheets of paper with ratchet marks on both long sides. He handed them to Mrs. Vanderwaal and then disappeared without uttering a word. "This is for you, dear," she said, separating the pages and tapping their sides until all the edges were even. "Your uncle was eloquent," she said as she handed them to me. "Absolutely eloquent. But, of course, it did no good. No good at all."

I put the Post-it on the top page of the transcript and got up to go. Mrs. Vanderwaal leaned in close and whispered in my ear, "In this town, my dear, the lawyers *always* win."

"But there's *always* a first time, Mrs. Vanderwaal."

"Right you are, my dear. I'm proud of you for trying. Don't forget to turn in your badge on your way out."

—the best monument

I found the same bench in Town Square. I sat down and read Uncle Alex's statement to the city council:

The city says that we built three tall structures without a permit. The city refers to them as *structures*. If you'll permit me, like everyone else, I'll call them *towers*.

The city says that without a building permit, the towers are illegal. And the city also says that we couldn't have gotten a permit unless we had a plan. The city says, "No plan, no permit."

Does it surprise you that every house in what you are calling Old Town was built without a permit? Look it up. You'll see. The Tappan Glass Works owned the land where they built our house and every house on Schuyler Place, and all the other houses in the neighborhood were built without permits. The glass factory built them for their workers, and they built them without permits because they owned the land, and they were the boss, and nobody was going to tell the boss what it could do and not do on its own land.

Now the city council has declared that the Glass houses are a zone. And the zone has a

144

code. When we started the towers, my brother and I, we had no zoning code—or zip code or area code, either, for that matter. We had an address: 19 Schuyler Place. And we had a neighborhood. We loved our neighborhood and everything in it—our houses and our streets paved with bricks in the herringbone pattern. We loved the chestnut trees that lined both sides of the street. The branches of the trees make a canopy from the odd-numbered side to the even. And we loved our backyards, too. Some of the backyards had vegetable gardens of cabbages and tomatoes. Some had gardens of hollyhocks and irises, and in one of those backyards there was a garden of towers. The neighbors shared the cabbages and hollyhocks and Mrs. Bevilaqua's tomatoes. Mrs. Bevilaqua's tomatoes were so special, we called them by the name *pomo d'oro,* "golden apples." The neighbors loved those tomatoes. The neighbors loved the towers too. You see, when we were a neighborhood, there was not a zoning code, there was an unwritten code. That unwritten code was: Love thy neighbor. But when we became a zone, we got a zoning code, which is written into law. And the city council says that the towers don't belong inside the zone because they don't fit the code.

Since we are now a zone and not a neighborhood, we also don't have neighbors. We have *home owners*. And just as the zone wrote a code, the home owners formed an *association*. The Home Owners Association. Very official. It has bylaws. The Home Owners Association says that the towers lower property values for the professionals who have bought these old houses as an investment. When the Glass Works put the houses up for sale, people like my brother and me, we bought these Glass houses to live in, not to invest in.

But now the Redevelopment Authority is saying something worse. The Redevelopment Authority is saying that the towers don't fit the history of Old Town. My brother and I wonder, How can anyone— any *authority*—have the authority to say that the towers are not part of history? How can anyone say that something that happened, didn't happen? My brother and I ask, Where does this history begin? The Redevelopment Authority answers that history begins with the first house in the Old Town *zone*. So then my brother and I ask, Where does history end? The Redevelopment Authority answers that history ends when the first permit begins. In other words, the history of Old Town begins when the Glass Works built the houses and ends when the towers begin.

How can you say that? History has no end. As soon as I say this word *history*, it is part of history.

No one should be allowed to take away someone's history. *No one.*

My brother and I ask you to do one thing: Don't take away the history of the towers. Instead, take a good look at it. And if you look, really look, you will see that the towers fit the times and the zone and that the history of the towers is part of the new Old Town.

I put the pages down and stared at the courthouse. *When you get older, édes Margitkám, you'll realize that all you have is time. You have time and your side of history. And that's all you have.* One by one, events of recent history fell into place.

The Uncles would not be building the fourth tower because it really would be a waste of time, and there never would be lemon and lime sherbet to go with the orange because all maintenance on the towers would be a waste of time too.

The Uncles had not wanted me to stay with them because they didn't want me to witness the destruction of the towers that I loved so much. And they couldn't bring themselves to tell me because they loved me too much.

And now Tartufo too made sense.

Uncle Alex didn't really care if Tartufo found a truffle. He had gone to Italy and bought Tartufo when all this legal wrangling started. He wanted someplace to go, something to do in the evenings when he would have been working on the towers. He didn't want Uncle Morris to approve of Tartufo or his truffle hunting. Like the path between their roses and peppers, the Uncles needed this difference to unite them.

And now the trip to Texas made sense too. They had gone there not because Uncle Alex wanted to prove that Tartufo could find a truffle or because Uncle Morris cared about the eight hundred dollars a pound that truffles might bring, but because they wanted to get out of town. They wanted to get away from the community that had cast them out. They did not prefer the *warm companionship* of the Home Owners Association and the *friendly guidance* of the city council.

fourteen

I stood on the even-numbered side of Schuyler Place and studied number 19. There was a slight breeze—too high and too slight to feel—but enough to make the pendants on the towers dance. Their sound floated above my head. Why didn't their music work for everyone?

I looked over at number 21, at the tasteful wooden sign that said

HAPGOOD, HAPGOOD & MARTIN

ATTORNEYS AT LAW

Hapgood had said that the towers were a blight on Old Town. He didn't like the towers because they lowered his property value. The story at number 17 was different. Gwendolyn and Geoffrey Klinger lived there, and they hated the towers because of me. It was my fault. Totally.

—The story at number 17

On the first day of spring vacation last year, I arrived at Schuyler Place and found Uncle Alex out in the yard pruning his roses. He called it editing. He always waited for the forsythia to bloom before he edited. He always said, "What you take away is as important as what you leave, Margitkám," and then he would add, "and what you take away makes what you leave more important."

Epiphany was far enough north that sometimes the forsythia came into bloom on dim, gray days when the skies and the temperature—everything except the calendar and the forsythia—said, *winter.* But on this, my first day of spring vacation, the air was so clear and the sky so bright that the forsythia seemed to cast a yellow halo in the air above it. I shaded my eyes with my hand as I watched Uncle edit his roses with pruning shears and a small saw.

Gwendolyn Klinger called to me over the fence and asked if she could talk to me about something. She always spoke just above a whisper, and she always made me feel as if I caused global warming by speaking too loud. So in her presence, as often as I could, I nodded.

"Can we go inside?" she whispered.

I nodded yes.

She sat down on the sofa in the Uncles' living room. Gwendolyn Klinger always wore sincere natural fibers and no makeup. I sat on a chair on the opposite side of the room and concentrated. She patted the sofa cushion next to her and said, "Come here, Margaret. I need to read your body language."

I did as requested. I sat so close to her that I saw the irises of her eyes whittle to pinpoints. I whispered, "What is it?"

"Margaret Rose," she said in her natural voice, which was not much louder than a whisper but was as moist as a French movie star's, "I know you are starting your spring vacation. I also know that you like to spend time with your uncles when you are out of school." I nodded, wondering where all this was leading. "Will you do me a favor?" Before I could answer, Gwendolyn reached out and took my hands and folded them into hers—like a hand sandwich. "For Geoffrey and me? This means as much to him as it does to me."

"What is it?" I asked, hushed, worried.

Unlike my uncles, who were in business together but separately and who ran the household together but separately, Gwendolyn and Geoffrey Klinger were as together as the biblical Ruth and Naomi, except they were of opposite gender. They were together in all endeavors. The law, remodeling their house, decorating their offices, cooking, baking. Everything. Gwendolyn said, "Geoffrey and I are going away for a week. There's a conference on torts in Tucson. . . ."

"There's a whole conference on tortes?" I asked,

allowing my voice to rise. I knew they liked to cook and bake, but I couldn't imagine two lawyers going all the way to Arizona to attend a conference on tortes. "Uncle Alex can probably teach you everything you need to know about tortes, Mrs. Klinger. He bakes a Dobos torte and a Sacher torte that could take a prize and—"

Gwendolyn Klinger smiled benevolently. "No, Margaret dear, these torts are T-O-R-T-S. They are legal cases, like when one person sues another for wrongful acts willfully done."

"I thought you meant the kind of cakes that are called tortes."

"I know you did, dear, but that has an *e* on the end. T-O-R-T-*E*," she said, at last unwrapping the hand sandwich so that she could pat my hand. I pulled both my hands away—slowly, so as to not cause any offense—and moved to the far end of the sofa. "Geoffrey and I thought we'd like to stay in Arizona a few extra days as a little vacation, but we need someone to take care of a little something for us. Will you?"

I wondered why a grown woman would say *little* so much, but I nodded yes.

Gwendolyn lowered her head and stretched her neck to read my body language. "Sure?" she asked.

Not at all sure I meant it, I said, "Sure."

She reached for my hand again, but I decided to twist my earring. (Getting my ears pierced had been my birthday present for turning ten.) I waited.

Gwendolyn said, "We need you to feed our starter. It's not like it will die if you don't, but it is very important to Geoffrey and me that you feed it. It's so new, so very new; it needs a little extra care."

"I think you ought to tell me what it is I'll be feeding."

Gwendolyn looked down at her lap and said, "It's our starter."

Well, I thought, if I heard right, she's talking about *starts*, not *stoats*, so it's probably not a ferret. I certainly hoped it wasn't a ferret. I had heard that some people were getting ferrets. I didn't want to feed a ferret. I also didn't want to feed a hamster or a gerbil or any variety of mouse. I didn't even like Mickey.

"We would like you to feed it once while we are gone. Only once. We would like you to do this for us. Will you?" she asked. "For Geoffrey and me?"

"I will if you tell me what a starter is."

"It's our flour-and-water mixture that contains the yeast used to make bread rise. Ours is a very famous starter. We sent to San Francisco for it. I haven't used it yet because it is still so new, but when I do use it, our bread will be sourdough."

"And you want me to feed it?"

She giggled girlishly and reached for my hand, which I had been keeping out of reach. "It's the yeast, silly. Yeast is a living organism. Yeast needs to be fed. It is a type of fungus, and it is used in fermenting bread to make it rise. Although the instructions say we can let our starter go for even a month without feeding it, it's new, and it is special. We don't want it to go so long. I saved its feeding for today, so if you'll come over to our house, I'll show you how."

We entered the back door of 17 Schuyler Place. The Klingers' was the first house on Schuyler Place to add on a room in the back to use as a living room. They had also completely renovated the kitchen, adding large windows along the back that captured the afternoon sun to warm and brighten the kitchen. It was the nicest room in the house. The countertops had more appliances than I had ever seen outside a Williams-Sonoma catalog. On a magnetic holder there was a full range of knives from small to large, like the bars of a xylophone, and hanging from an overhead rack were pans in more shapes than you would find in a geometry book.

From her refrigerator, Gwendolyn took a pint-size jar that had a rubber gasket and a metal clamp to keep it sealed. She opened the jar, and a sour smell filled the room. I winced, but Gwendolyn seemed not to notice. I coughed. "Can you tell me what that is on top?" I asked, pointing to a ditchwater-dark liquid that floated on top of the jar.

Gwendolyn smiled. "It's called *hootch*," she said. "It's the liquid that comes from the fermentation. Yeast is also used to make beer and wine." Then, with loving patience, she showed me how to feed a starter. With every step, she refined the instructions with a running commentary of do's and don't's. When she stirred the mixture with a wooden spoon, she warned, "Never use a metal spoon with yeast." She kept up a low hum of conversation as she slowly, slowly blended in the liquid until the mixture started to froth. She carefully, carefully measured out a cup full of the frothing mixture and washed it down her disposal. As she rinsed out and dried the measuring cup, she told me, "We don't use tap water. It's too chlorinated." Telling me to make certain that the bottom of the meniscus is at the one-cup line when held at eye-level, she poured bottled water—not too cold, not too hot—into the cup and then into the jar and followed that with a cup of white powdery stuff from a canister marked FARINE but that looked like flour to me. She stirred the mixture with the wooden spoon again and covered the jar with a dishtowel. "We allow it to sit at room temperature for a little while so that the new ingredients can communicate with the old before we cap it and return it to the refrigerator." She handed me the key to her back door. "We would like you to come over Friday and do this for us. Just this once." She folded her hands as if in prayer and asked, "Will you?"

I nodded.

"Do you have any questions?"

I didn't want to have one, but I did. "What's meniscus?" I asked.

"The convex upper surface of a liquid."

"And that's to be at the one-cup line?"

"The bottom of it is. That is, the bottom of the curve of the meniscus is to be at the one-cup mark."

"When at eye-level," I said.

"Yes, at eye-level," she repeated. And then she asked, "Would you like me to write out the directions?"

"No, thank you," I said.

"Would you mind repeating them?"

"Yes," I replied.

"Well?"

I pursed my lips, raised my eyebrows, and stretched my neck toward her so that she could read my body language. I said nothing.

"Oh," she said, smiling awkwardly. "You feel you already know them?"

I nodded.

• • •

The weather had held that whole week. By Friday, Uncle Alex was worried that his roses would set buds too soon and be nipped by a late freeze. I fed the starter at midmorning and went back to Uncle's, where we had an early lunch, after which I mixed up the paint that became known as orange sherbet. Uncle Alex supervised, which made him late for the Time Zone. He called Uncle Morris and told him he was running late and asked me to walk Tartufo while he cleaned up for work. The sun that had warmed us all day was high and hot as I put Tartufo on the leash and sauntered over to the Klingers' to put the starter back in the refrigerator.

The kitchen door was not even all the way open when I knew that something was wrong. It stank. I thought I would pass out or throw up. Before I could catch my breath, Tartufo darted past me and was licking hootch off the floor. Splinters of glass were sprinkled over a moonscape of farine paste. Puddles of hootch were everywhere.

Tartufo was racing around the kitchen, slipping on all fours, licking the floor and scattering mounds of gray-looking farine. He was getting wild. I had to get him out of there. Slipping and sliding and using words I had only read in banned books, I made my way over to Tartufo and managed to grab him by the collar. He would not budge. He had been trained for years to hunt the musty smell of truffles. What a time for his training to kick in!

"Stop it!" I yelled. "Stop it now!" But Tartufo was in hootch heaven. He was licking the floor clean. I knew that he was already feeling no pain, even—God forbid!—the pain of swallowing glass.

I made my way back across the slippery kitchen floor and ran to Uncle's house. Fortunately, Uncle Alex had not yet left for work. He recognized panic when he saw it. He ran next door with me. He entered first and quietly sneaked up behind Tartufo and grabbed him by his hindquarters. Tartufo looked back at Uncle very briefly—I think he snarled—and returned to lapping up the foul-smelling stuff—liquid and paste. His paws made a sucking sound as Uncle lifted him up off the floor.

When we returned to 19 Schuyler Place, Tartufo started running around the kitchen. Around and around. "He's drunk," Uncle said.

"Should we give him black coffee?"

"Couldn't hurt," Uncle replied. Handing me the leash, he told me, "Try to get him to walk it off."

I took him around the block, tugging on the leash to make him keep going. His stomach was swollen, and the skin on his underbelly, which was never a thing of beauty, looked like an uncooked egg roll that a sloppy chef had dribbled with soy sauce. When I got back,

Uncle Alex was brewing coffee. (This was a household where instant coffee was not allowed. Uncle Morris said that he spit on it.)

Tartufo curled up in his corner, farted three times, and fell asleep.

"Do you think he will be all right?" I asked, worried.

"Wake him and keep him moving," Uncle replied. He looked down at his trousers and shirt. The farine was starting to dry like splotches of Portland cement. "As soon as the coffee brews, cool some down and see if you can get him to drink some. I've got to go upstairs and clean up. Please call your uncle and tell him that I missed the bus."

Uncle Morris started every day a little bit irritated with his brother. This would be the second call about Uncle Alex's being late. On a normal one-call day when Alex missed his bus, Morris would explode. I had had enough explosions for the day, so I began by saying, "Uncle Morris, this is Margaret, and I've made a terrible mistake."

It wasn't until I reviewed for him what I had done that I realized that I had skipped one step. In the mass of sub-instructions about meniscuses and eye-levels, I had forgotten to put a tea towel over the jar while the starter communicated. I had screwed the lid back on too soon. The sun beating in through the Klingers' bright, sunny windows had made the gases build up pressure and caused the jar to burst.

Uncle Morris said, "Don't worry. It was a mistake. I'll wait here until Alex comes. As soon as he arrives, I'll come home to help." Before he hung up, he asked, "Is Tartufo okay?"

"He's sleeping it off."

By the time I felt it was safe to leave Tartufo, the flour paste had hardened and stuck to the spotless Klinger floors. Uncle Morris was home by then, so he and I put wet paper towels over the globs to moisten them so that we could scrape them off without causing damage to the floor. It took hours.

I insisted on the Uncles giving me an advance on my allowance so that I would be responsible for paying for a new starter and for Federal Express delivery, but, it did not arrive until after Geoffrey and Gwendolyn had returned from their Arizona torts. I went over to their house with the new starter and an apology. When I told them the part about Tartufo, they didn't laugh.

"I skipped a step," I explained.

"If you remember, Margaret, I had volunteered to write them down, and I did ask you to review the procedure."

"I remember."

"Then you would say it was negligence?"

"But not willfully done. I did not do it on purpose. I

made a mistake," I insisted. "I didn't mean to kill your starter, and I am sorry about it. If my apology and cleaning up the damage and buying you this new starter aren't enough, you'll have to tort me."

Geoffrey laughed unpleasantly. "No, no," he said. He examined the starter that I had brought over. "This is from the same place we got ours, Gwennie. What do you say we just start over?"

Gwennie nodded and murmured, "I *had* asked her to repeat the instructions."

I left.

Neither Gwendolyn nor Geoffrey had asked how Tartufo was doing.

Later that spring when the Uncles did due maintenance on the towers—after they had painted the towers with my orange-sherbet paint—Geoffrey Klinger called the towers an "off-color joke." Uncle Alex said to him, "The towers themselves are a joke, Mr. Klinger. They would be useless if they weren't." To which Geoffrey Klinger replied, "You and I have very different definitions of *useless.*" To which Uncle Alex replied, "And jokes."

—time and your side of history
As I stood across the street and looked at the Klingers' own tastefully painted sign, I wished that Geoffrey and

Gwendolyn had gone to Arizona to study tortes instead of torts. They undoubtedly suffered from OCD, obsessive-compulsive disorder. Such people are to be pitied. But the Klingers were only part of the problem. The full weight of the treachery belonged to the Home Owners Association of Old Town and the Redevelopment Authority. The Klingers were enemies only because they were part of them. What made the home owners and the redevelopment people think they had the right to destroy something that had been part of the town for longer than they had been?

I had defined the enemy. I was prepared to fight.

It would be me against them, just as it had been me against the Alums. But there was this important difference: I would be fighting to save something other than my own sweet self.

—When you get older, *édes* **Margitkám**
In only one day, I had already gotten much older.

—you realize that all you have is time
I checked my digital watch. I had four and a half hours before Uncle Morris returned. Four and a half hours that were all my own. Four and a half hours to think and eight and a half days to take action.

—You have time and your side of history

I didn't have much time, but there was forty-five years of history on my side.

—And that's all you have

But that was not all I had. I also had two of the three steps it would take to change things.

The first step was being unhappy with things the way they were. I already had that step well behind me. I was more than unhappy. I was pissed.

The second step was having a desire to change things. Well, I was there already. I was burning with desire to change things.

The third step was having a plan.

Unfortunately, that was still in my future.

Uncle Alex had said that you can't stop history from happening because the entire past tense is history. But the future is choices. And the choices of a single person can change future history even if that person is under-age and does not have a driver's license or a credit card. I thought about Joan of Arc (but not her fate) and Anne Frank (but not her fate either).

As soon as I had a plan, I was ready to change history.

fifteen

The minute I got back to the house, I dialed the number that Mrs. Vanderwaal had given me. I expected to get an answering machine but got a human voice instead. Unprepared, I asked, "Who is this?"

A pleasant male voice answered, "This is Peter." Pause. "Now, who are you?"

"I am Margaret Rose Kane," I began, and then I rattled on. "I am the daughter of Naomi Landau, who is the daughter of Margaret Rose Landau, who was the sister of Morris and Alexander Rose. They were your neighbors when you lived at 21 Schuyler Place. I am their grandniece, Margaret Rose, and we need to talk."

"Can we start at the beginning? Please?" Peter Vanderwaal had lightly dusted his native Epiphany accent with the vowels of the British royal family. But there was also something welcoming and kind in his voice. "This sounds like a matter of some urgency."

"Very urgent," I said.

"Because?"

"It is urgent because the towers are coming down

unless we can save them." I heard him gasp. I began reading him the newspaper article. He interrupted when I had gotten no further than *"The city has awarded the contract to demolish the structures to—"* He asked me to repeat what I had just read.

". . . demolish the structures . . ."

"Aha!" he said. "Their first mistake."

"Which is?"

"Structures," he said. "That's where we'll get them."

"Where is that, Mr. Vanderwaal?"

"The towers are not structures. They are important works of outsider art."

"Does *outsider art* mean that it isn't indoors?"

"No, no, my dear. *Outsider art* means art that is *outside* the mainstream."

I wondered, Didn't his Ivy League college teach him that you shouldn't define a word with the word being defined?

Mr. Peter Vanderwaal continued, "Most people call it *folk* art. It means it was done by a person who has not been formally trained."

I had heard the towers called an "off-color joke" and "superfluous" and "a waste of time," but I had never heard them called works of art. "You mean that my uncles are artists?"

"Yes, Margaret Rose, I do mean that. They fit the

category: Outsider artists make up their own techniques and use materials that trained artists don't use. That's your uncles. Outsider art is less refined, less restrained than mainstream art—there is always something untamed about it. An outsider artist is like a gypsy violinist. Either you are a gypsy violinist or you aren't. You don't—you can't—go to school to become one. And that's the towers."

"And that means that the towers are works of art?"

"Precisely. Your uncles are artists, and the towers are not structures that were built without permits or plans. They are true works of art. They are, in fact, masterpieces."

Masterpieces, I thought. My uncles made masterpieces. There were three of them in the backyard of 19 Schuyler Place. Ten minutes ago, I didn't even know they were artists, and now Peter Vanderwaal had said they are masterpiece artists. "Mr. Vanderwaal," I asked, "are you sure that my uncles are artists?"

"I'm sure."

"And the towers are masterpieces?"

"They are. But, Margaret, I suggest you recover from this shocking bit of news so that we can discuss the problem at hand. But first, I must hear the remaining portion of the article. Read on." When I was done, he asked, "Does your mother know about this impending doom?"

"She does, but she can't help. She's off on an archaeological dig."

"Really? How very interesting. I've always wanted to do that myself. Is it Egypt?"

"Peru."

"Oh, yes, of course. Egypt wouldn't do. There's that Jewish thing." Mr. Vanderwaal paused a minute and then asked, "Your uncles haven't put Stars of David or anything religious on top of those towers, have they?"

"No. Just the clock faces."

"Yes, yes," Peter Vanderwaal said. "Totally secular. None of the neighbors ever objected when we strung Christmas lights all over the towers. One year my dad wired up a Rudolph the Red-Nosed Reindeer atop one of the towers. Of course, Rudolph is not in any way religious, although one could—if he were hell-bent on objecting—make a case that it had to do with Christmas and therefore was. You don't suppose the neighbors are anti-Semites, do you?"

"No, they're lawyers."

"That, my dear Margaret Rose, is the problem right there."

"They say they're worried about safety."

"Pish posh," said Peter Vanderwaal. "Those towers are safe. I climbed each one of them to the tippy-top every Christmas I lived there, and I can assure you I am no athlete, *and* I have a very protective mother, and no one ever worried about my safety. Those towers are safe, my dear. They were built one rung at a time. Each part was made to fit tight and right before the next was added. They are what we call *modular*. The rungs are only as far apart as your uncles could reach, and neither is very tall. The towers could and did support the weight of both your uncles at the same time, and I suppose you've noticed, neither of your uncles is underweight."

"They do put real cream in their coffee, Mr. Vanderwaal."

"Very civilized, but irrelevant to the matter at hand." He thought a minute. "But this isn't: Those towers have been through windstorms that blew down mighty oaks and ice storms that cracked cables as thick as my wrist, and nothing ever happened to the towers except some of the pendants came off. I can assure anyone who asks that if the forces of nature have not blown them down, nothing ever will. Those towers were built to last. It will take a blast of dynamite to take them down. Surely they're not going to risk dynamiting them—or are they?"

"One report says that they will be *deconstructed* from the top down. Eddie Foscaro says that he cannot chop them down like redwoods because there is no place for them to fall, and he can't implode them because they are too close to the other houses."

Peter Vanderwaal thought a minute more. "Let me tell you something, Margaret Rose. This travesty the Home Owners Association is trying to pull off is really about money. Those old Glass houses are not homes to those yuppies. They are investments. Fixing them up is nothing more than a chance to get money from that trust fund and resell them at a profit. What the lawyers are saying is that their property values will go up if their idea of historical accuracy prevails. Make no mistake about it. The only thing more destructive than someone who thinks his idea is the only possible correct one is a group of people who all think they and only they have the right answer. And when that group is lawyers, watch out."

He paused only long enough to catch his breath. "We have to do something to stop this cultural Armageddon." He took another breath. "If we can just stop the demolition until I can get something together to prove that the towers are not structures but works of art, I think we'll have a shot at saving them."

"Do you have a plan?"

"I'm going to do the first two things grown-ups do when they are faced with a problem."

"What are they, Mr. Vanderwaal?"

"One, they form a committee; and two, they give that committee a name."

"Okay," I said. "What will they name the committee?"

"Not *they*. Naming the committee is very important, so *we* will name the committee. I suggest we call our committee the Cultural Preservation Committee. Yes. That name is very good. It has two out of three positive words: *cultural* and *preservation*. Everyone in the world is in favor of culture and preservation, and everyone in the world has to live with committees."

"The Cultural Preservation Committee," I repeated.

"Yes. We'll abbreviate it CPC. Which is also very good. We don't want an acronym. Acronyms are so over."

"So who will be on your committee? My uncles?"

"No, no, no, Margaret Rose. Forgive me, but your uncles must stay out of it completely. But completely. Your uncles must never show by the least scintilla that they care. They must be artfully indifferent."

"That won't be hard. They seem to have given up. I think they're resigned to the towers coming down, but I know someone who will be happy to join the CPC. His name is Jacob Kaplan, and he's an artist, and he admires the towers a lot."

"Who is that?"

I welcomed an opportunity to repeat the name. "Jacob Kaplan. He's an artist, and he loves the towers, and he's going to paint a rose on the ceiling of my bedroom. He'll be happy to join the CPC."

"Good," Peter said, "that'll be fine. But we need rainmakers—people who are known to make things happen. People with prestige. People from the world of art who can get results. I know some. I'll sign them up. I have some pictures of the towers that I took at various stages of their completion."

"Your mother has a picture of you and my mother and Loretta Bevilaqua on the towers. Won't that show how safe they are?"

"Maybe. But that won't be the angle I'll be working. I shall get a group together to have the towers declared works of art. My group, of course, will be known as *consultants*."

"Will you be forming a committee of consultants?"

"Margaret Rose, my dear, no such thing as a committee of consultants exists. Consultants have been known to work *with* committees and even, on occasion, *on* a committee, but they never *form* committees for the simple reason that each believes his opinion carries so much weight, you could not possibly need more than one. So, my dear Margaret Rose, I must gather their opinions one at a time."

"What angle will I be working?"

"I'm glad you asked. Here's the first, second, and third thing you must do: One, stop the demolition. Two, stop the demolition. Three, stop the demolition."

"How?"

"Any way you can. When is it to start?"

"Next week."

"So you see how important your job is?"

I saw Uncle Morris's car pulling into the alley. "I'll think of something, Mr. Vanderwaal," I said. "I've got to go now."

"Stay in touch," he said.

"You, too," I replied, and hung up just seconds before Uncle Morris walked through the door.

sixteen

After my uncles went upstairs to assemble the scaffold, I found the name *Bevilaqua* in the phone book. There was only one. I waited to call until after the sounds of my uncles' arguing stopped, and the clang of metal being joined to metal punctuated the sound of Mozart coming from my bedroom radio.

I had not expected a lengthy conversation with Mrs. Bevilaqua. All I really wanted was to find out how to reach her daughter, but Mrs. Bevilaqua was lonely, curious, and proud of her daughter. So she asked a lot of questions about my mother, my father, and my uncles. She insisted on knowing why I wanted to get in touch with Loretta, and when I told her, she said, "Oh, yeah, my Loretta loved them towers. Especially at Christmas. She helped decorate them. Your mother did, too. All the neighborhood decorated them towers. Even that chubby Vanderwaal kid, Peter, a boy."

—Especially at Christmas
The year that Tower One was finished and the Uncles had set the foundation for Tower Two, the Bevilaquas and the Vander-

waals asked if they could hang Christmas lights on Tower One. Christmas was not the Uncles' holiday to celebrate, but the spirit of the season was, so they said yes, and that started the holiday lights tradition. Everyone—including my mother—helped decorate the towers.

When the second tower went up—long before it was at its full height—it, too, was decorated, and in the years that followed, decorating and lighting the towers became a neighborhood project. On a designated night, John Flanagan, who was a policeman and a neighbor, set up barricades and closed off Schuyler Place from Melville to Rinehart Streets, and all the neighbors gathered in that one block and sang carols and drank mulled cider and ate doughnuts. And then Mr. Vanderwaal, who was an electrician, threw a switch, and the tower lights went on.

The tradition of the Christmas lights continued even after the Bevilaquas left the neighborhood. The last year of the block party, the Epiphany Times ran a feature article on holiday decorations, and the towers made the front page of the style section. They were considered a sight worth seeing. Even people who by then normally avoided the area after dark drove by to see the tower lights. City buses slowed down to let the people get a good look.

It was not until the year after I was born that the tradition of the Christmas block party died. The Vanderwaals and the Bevilaquas had long since moved away, and by that time, their children, Loretta and Peter, had left Epiphany altogether.

• • •

I asked Mrs. Bevilaqua if she would please give me Loretta's phone number. She said, "My Loretta, she's a big shot with Infinitel. You heard of Infinitel, eh?"

I said that I had watched their commercials on TV. "They're the telephone company that has the motto, *We go the distance for you*, aren't they?"

Mrs. Bevilaqua said, "That's right. That's the one." Then she repeated the motto and told me that Loretta was in charge of Infinitel's PCS, their Personal Communication Services division, which was their new division for wireless phones. "She has a big office in a corner of one of them tall buildings in New York. She has windows that see a river on one side and a bridge on the other—both going to somewheres in Brooklyn." Mrs. Bevilaqua told me that Loretta had married a man named Homer Smith. "She don't use *Smith* in her business. For business she stays a Bevilaqua. Anyways, she divorced that *Smith*. So she's still a Bevilaqua anyways. The company, they don't want her to use Smith. Whenever them big shots at Infinitel hear *Bevilaqua*, they know it means something."

I asked if I could please have a number to reach Loretta.

"You want home or business?"

"Both, if I may."

"At work she has a secretary, called an *administray assist*. He's not a woman neither. He's a man, her administray assist. He don't let nobody get on line unless they mean business. Big business. He asks, 'Who I'm gonna say is calling, please?' Very polite, but he don't let nobody get on. But Loretta, she has two more lines in the office. One just for Infinitel people to talk to her. *Intracom*, it's called. I say, why not have three phones? They can afford it. That's their business, anyways. And she got the administray assist to keep track. Now I'll get you the number. Hold the phone."

When Mrs. Bevilaqua returned to the line, she gave me two numbers—one for work and one for home. "This home number I'm giving you is a unlisted number. It's very private, which means that nobody gets it unless I give it. *Capisci?*"

Cah-PEESH-ee? I guessed that Mrs. Bevilaqua was asking if I understood. I shook my head yes. Mrs. Bevilaqua asked again, *"Capisci?"*

"Yes, yes, I understand. I understand completely."

"What do you understand?"

"That I'm not to bother her unless it is important. Really important."

"Yes. *Capisci*." After giving me the two numbers, area code first, Mrs. Bevilaqua advised me to call Loretta at home in the evening, or "you won't get past the administray assist." I thanked her, and she said, "Loretta, she liked them towers, anyways. Me too. Especially at Christmas."

I decided that since it was already evening, immediately would be the best time to call Loretta Bevilaqua.

Loretta herself answered after only three rings. I introduced myself the same way I had introduced myself to Peter Vanderwaal, mentioning my mother and my uncles.

Loretta asked, "How *are* they?"

I told her that my mother was in Peru and that my uncles were depressed. She asked me why, so I brought her up-to-date on the sad recent history of the towers. She listened all the way through without interrupting, and then she said, "Legality would be the first thing the lawyers would work on. By declaring the towers illegal, they get the law on their side; and by having the neighborhood declared a landmark, they can claim that they have improved the value of your uncles' property. What would make their property values go up even more would be to restore the neighborhood to what it was before the towers were built. The neighborhood is not as old as Williamsburg, but—"

"Uncle Morris spits on Williamsburg. He says that it may be accurate, but it is not true. He says it gives new meaning to the phrase *real phony.*"

"But Old Town would be much more true. The buildings would not be reconstructed. They would be restored. Old Town would not be a walk-around museum like Williamsburg. It would be a living community like Rainbow Row in Charleston. By declaring the neighborhood a historical treasure, your uncles' property value goes up along with all the others."

"Peter Vanderwaal says that the towers are an *artistic* treasure."

"Peter Vanderwaal? You've talked to Peter?"

"I have."

"When?"

"Today."

"How is he?"

"He's fine. He says that the only values these lawyers and home owners know are property values. *Their* property values. They care about profit, not art, and Peter Vanderwaal says that the towers are art. Outsider art. They are my uncles' personal expression, and my uncles have the right to express themselves. Freedom of expression is part of the law."

"And so is something called the 'commonweal'—the welfare of the community. Some years ago, an artist by the name of Christo—a Bulgarian—put up something he called *Running Fence,* which was twenty-four and a half miles of a white curtain running up and down the

California hills north of San Francisco into the ocean. It took him forty-two months and eighteen public hearings—"

"My uncles never had hearings—"

"—and permission from fifty-nine ranchers—"

"My uncles didn't know they needed permission—"

"—to approve his plans—"

"My uncles never had plans—"

"—and a four-hundred-fifty-page environmental impact report—"

"My uncles never impacted the environment, just the neighborhood—"

"—and bore all the expense to put it up."

"My uncles never asked anyone for a penny."

"And two weeks after completing the fence, he took it down. Today, no sign of *Running Fence* remains on the face of the land." I thought about that for a long time until Loretta asked, "Margaret? Are you still there?"

"I'm still here," I answered. "And this is what I have to say about forty-two months. Forty-two months is a lot different from forty-five years. And here is what I have to say about taking down *Running Fence*. Taking it down was part of it. Taking it down was an important part of its history, but that's not so for the towers. My uncles never meant for the towers to come down.

They're not even all finished. My uncles were ready to start a fourth tower, but they never did."

"Speaking of fences, will they let your uncles keep the fence?"

"Yes. None of the fence shows from the street. Which goes to show that they not as interested in the commonweal as they are in appearances."

"Would they let your uncles keep the towers if they removed the sections that peek over the top of the buildings?"

I was shocked. "I wouldn't even ask," I said. "That would . . . that would destroy the whole . . . the whole . . . *majesty* of them." I had never used the word *majesty* before. It came from some deep, knowing, inside part of me. Words can be part of your soul before they are part of your vocabulary. The thought that my mother's old friend was taking the other side was making me sick. She was making me sick. "Are you a lawyer?" I asked.

"Yes, I am. I started at Infinitel in the legal department."

"Now I know why you're on their side."

"Whose side are we talking about?"

"*Theirs!* The lawyers and the home owners who live all around my uncles."

"I'm sorry that's what you think."

"Well, I do."

"Your thinking is wrong. I do love the towers, and I am going to save them. Now tell me what Peter said."

"He said he'll form a committee, the Cultural Preservation Committee. He's going to get signatures from important art authority rainmakers on a petition to have the towers declared a landmark. We're going to call it the CPC because acronyms are so over."

Loretta laughed.

"He didn't laugh at me."

"Neither am I. I am laughing at Peter. It's so like him to form a committee. Rainmaker art authorities! That's an oxymoron." She laughed again. "And what are you going to do?"

"I'm to keep them from destroying the towers in the meantime."

"Now, that," Loretta said, "is sound advice. That's what I recommend, too. Stop them from destroying the towers until I can save them."

"How are you going to save them?"

"I can't tell you yet. I have a lot of behind-the-scenes work to do first. We will have a three-phase plan."

"We?" I asked suspiciously. Was this another royal *we*?

"Yes. You, Peter, and me. Phase One: Stop. Phase Two: Stall. Phase Three: Save. You are the most important player in Phase One. You must stop the demolition."

"How do I do that?"

"Listen, Margaret, I am willing to work on saving the towers, and I am willing to lay out a plan, but I do not micromanage. *Capisci?*"

"Yes, *capisci.*"

"No. *Capisci* means *You understand.*"

"I do."

"Do what?"

"Understand."

"If you understand, you must say *capisco*. Cah-PISS-co. That means *I understand.*"

"I already told you. I understand."

Loretta Bevilaqua groaned audibly. "Then you understand that you must stop the demolition?"

"Yes."

"After you've stopped them, Peter and his petition from the CPC will tie their hands for a while and slow up the legal work long enough for me to start Phase Three, saving the towers." She paused only briefly before adding, "In order for me to complete my part— or even to begin it—you must buy the towers."

"I can't afford that."

"Yes, you can. Have your uncles sell them to you for a dollar."

"A piece?"

"All right, a dollar a piece."

"They are worth a lot more than that."

"Of course they are. Actually, they are priceless. That is why I want to save them. Pay whatever you want to for them. The important thing is that you become the owner. The law understands ownership. Until someone from the government serves you with a court order that the towers are to come down, you own them. As long as you own the towers, anyone who tries to occupy them without your permission is a trespasser. Possession is nine points of the law."

"Nine points out of how many?"

Quickly dismissing the question as unworthy of further thought, she said, "It doesn't matter. Get a bill of sale and have it notarized."

"Where do I do that?"

"Wherever there is a notary public. I told you, I strategize, I plan, but I do not micromanage. I'll get started on my part the first thing in the morning. Remember, if you want to save the towers, you must buy them and stop the demolition."

"I definitely want to save them."

"So do I."

Driving up the stakes, I added, "I *need* them."

"So do I," Loretta Bevilaqua replied, and quickly added, "So do we all."

She hung up before I could even say good-bye. Loretta was used to getting in the last word.

—**Whenever them big shots at Infinitel hear** *Bevilaqua*, **they know it means something.**
And so did I.

seventeen

It was almost midnight when the phone rang. My uncles were still working on the scaffold. Uncle Morris picked up the upstairs phone before I picked up the downstairs one. It was Jacob Kaplan. Stagestruck, I did not even say hello.

Jake said, "I'm sorry to be calling so late, but when I tried to call earlier, the line was busy."

"You must have had the wrong number," Morris said. "Nobody here was on the phone. I don't use the phone."

"You're using it now."

"An accident of proximity." In my mind I could see Uncle Alex trapped on top of the scaffold, forcing Uncle Morris to answer.

Jake was saying, "I called the operator and had her check the number. She confirmed that the line was busy."

Morris said, "It was Tartufo." Then, still holding the phone, he called to his brother, "That dog of yours knocked the phone off the receiver."

I heard Uncle Alex reply, "Couldn't be the dog."

Then Uncle Morris called downstairs, "Margaret, would you come up here a minute, please?"

I had not hung up, so I said into the phone, "What is it, Uncle?"

"Where are you?" Uncle Morris asked.

"Downstairs."

"Why do you sound so close?"

"I'm on the phone."

Morris said, "I thought this was Jake on the phone."

Jake said, "It is."

"It's both of us, Uncle. I'm on the extension."

"Say hello to Jake, Margitkám," Uncle Morris said.

"Hello, Jake," I said, and my heart did a grand jeté.

"Tell me, Margitkám, did Tartufo take the phone off the stand?"

I hated telling a lie. I hated blaming Tartufo—especially to Uncle Morris—but I could not tell the truth. "He did. I didn't notice it until a minute ago."

Morris turned away from the phone and said, "What did I tell you? It was your mongrel."

"Tartufo is not a mongrel. He's registered."

"He should never have been allowed into the country."

"Morris!" Uncle Alex said. "Find out what the young man wants. He didn't call long distance to hear

187

you insult my animal. Do you think he's paying Ma Bell for you to argue with me?"

"I'm not on Ma Bell," Jake said. "I use Infinitel for long distance."

"And you're going to tell me that they don't charge?"

"They do."

"So what is it that you want?"

"I want to tell you that I will be there about nine o'clock tomorrow morning and that I am six foot one inches tall, so please don't set the scaffold too high."

"All right," Morris said. "We'll be ready."

"See you soon," Jake said, and my heart, which had sped up even more from lying, slowed down enough for me to catch my breath and say:

"Good night, Jake."

I went upstairs. Welcoming an opportunity—any opportunity—to say his name, I said, (as casually as I could), "I knew Jake was tall, but I didn't know he was over six feet." To a family of modestly sized males, he was a giant.

Uncle Morris said, "What does he mean, not to set the scaffold too high? I thought he would be painting on his back. Like Michelangelo in that chapel."

Uncle Alex said, "Maybe he doesn't want to have his elbows akimbo."

"What means *akimbo*?"

"It means bent."

Uncle Morris persisted, "So how can you paint without bending an elbow? When we paint, our elbows bend."

"Maybe he means to be sitting."

"So listen. He's here early tomorrow. Before work we can adjust the scaffold to a quarter inch of how he wants it."

Uncle Alex said, "It will be exactly how he wants it. Exactly."

"That's what I said. Exactly."

"To within a quarter inch," Uncle Alex repeated.

"Did I say *a quarter inch*?" Uncle Morris asked.

"You did. So did I."

"I said it first."

"A quarter inch it is," Uncle Alex replied.

Uncle Morris turned his back to his brother and said, "I'm going to bed."

I laughed to myself. There's more than one way to get in the last word.

eighteen

I had been up since seven, waiting since eight. At a quarter to nine, I brewed a fresh pot of the special blend of coffee that Uncle Alex ordered from the Dean & Deluca catalog, which was where he had learned the price of truffles. I set the table for four and had the cream in a Herend pitcher chilling in the refrigerator. Next to the place where Jacob was to sit, I put the library book, opened to the rose rose I had selected. I had visions of sitting across the table from him, asking, *Would you care for a little more coffee?* and then having an extremely knowledgeable conversation about outsider art.

As soon as Jake arrived, Uncle Morris whisked him upstairs to examine the scaffold to see if it needed adjustment. It was, Jake decided, exactly the right height: masterfully built and designed. The struts were X-shaped, which gave it added strength and stability, and they were placed at close enough intervals that he could climb to the top as easily as he could climb a

flight of stairs. Jake said, "Perfect. It doesn't need anything more—it is perfect."

Uncle Morris said, "That's all I needed to hear." Of
course, that was not *all* he needed to hear. *Perfect* was *the
least* he needed. *Perfect* suited him just fine.

I invited Jake to come downstairs and have a cup of
coffee before he started work. I watched him close his
eyes and inhale deeply of its aroma. I waited as he added
cream and sugar and took his first long sip. I was hoping
he would say, *Perfect,* but he didn't. Just as I was beginning to think that he would never look at the book of
roses, he did. From the bib pocket of his white painter's
overalls, he took the slip of paper with the room dimen-
sions, a small ruler, and a pocket calculator. With the
ruler, he measured the rose I had selected. He did a few
rapid calculations. "Works out pretty well," he said.

I was worried. Could I have gotten a *perfect* instead of
a *pretty well* if I had chosen the Redouté?

Then, looking at Uncle Alex, he said, "If you will
help me with the preliminary work on the ceiling, I
may even be ready to start the painting today. Would
you mind?"

"Of course not," Uncle replied. "I much prefer helping to just sitting around."

"Do you know where there's a color copier? I will

need two copies of this page. They should be able to copy it double size."

Uncle had to think. Finally, he thought of the office supply store two blocks from the courthouse. He looked the number up in the phone book and called.

"They can do it," he said when he hung up.

"How much?" Jake asked. "I'm just curious."

"Twelve ninety-five each," Uncle said.

"I could make do with one. The second is backup."

"Always have a backup. I believe everyone should always have a backup. Besides, twenty-five dollars and ninety cents is not much for raw material for a work of art." He took a sheet of notepaper from the counter by the telephone and marked the place in the book before closing it. "I'll drop it off on my way to the mall and have Morris pick it up on his way home. He'll be home after six."

"Let me go," I said. "I, too, prefer helping to just sitting around."

"Good," Jake said. "I always like to know what you prefer." I was embarrassed but pleased. "Now, Margaret, if you'll pour me another cup of that excellent coffee before you leave, I'll take it upstairs and get started."

Jake climbed up and down the scaffold, moving it along like an old lady with a walker. He measured off the ceiling in six-inch intervals on both sides. He had to fudge a little so that there would be an even number of squares.

After he finished making his marks along two perimeters, he and Uncle each held the end of the piece of chalked string that Jake unwound from a small reel. When Jake was certain that the string was taut, he asked, "Ready?" And when Uncle answered, "Ready," Jake snapped it so that it left a blue line from one marker to its mate across the room. They went from marker to marker, making parallel lines. Then they turned ninety degrees, so that they could make lines perpendicular to those they had just finished.

By the time I returned from picking up the color copies, they had finished and both men were sweating profusely. Uncle Alex had to take a shower and get ready for work.

Before he even looked at the color copies, Jake wrapped a red bandanna around his forehead to keep the sweat out of his eyes. "Do you think you could find an electric fan somewhere?" he asked.

Coffee. Fan. I was happy to be his gofer.

I knew there was a fan in the unused dining room. I found it in a box behind the old display counter that Uncle Alex had used during the time that Jewels Bi-Rose had operated out of 19 Schuyler Place. It was dusty, of course. Everything in the unused dining room was. I picked the fan up and decided to test it before I cleaned it up and carried it upstairs. I began looking for a wall socket. The house was over sixty years old and, at best, had one outlet per wall.

Crawling behind the old display counter, I bumped into another box. I opened the flaps, and a fog of dust dimmed my view. I waved my hand in front of my face and sneezed at least three times before I could see what was inside. There were the handcuffs, the ones my uncles had kept handy for the crooks. The key was looped onto the chain with a piece of string. Deeper in the box was the roll of duct tape and the clean (but now dusty) socks for gags. I had to smile when I remembered that night before last when the Uncles had laughed as they told Jake about how they had learned to help the robbers in order to spare themselves.

I pushed the box aside and continued creeping along the floor, looking for a wall socket. I found one across the room under the front windows.

The fan worked. I cleaned it in the kitchen and carried it upstairs. Jake was sitting on the scaffold, looking over the tattersall of blue lines on the aged white of the ceiling. He clapped his hands together to shake the blue chalk dust from them.

I pointed to the empty socket in the center of the

ceiling where Jake had taken down the glass shade and had unscrewed the lightbulb. "What are you going to do there?" I asked.

"Look at the picture," he said. I did as told. "See where the center comes?" I nodded. Then he said, "On the plain glazed surface of this old glass shade, there will appear the succulent heart of the rose."

I gasped. "Does that mean that the succulent heart of the rose will be lit up whenever I turn on the light?" I asked.

"It means just that."

I grew faint at the thought. "It also means that I will have a glass ceiling after all." Even if Jake didn't say it, I knew I had chosen the perfect rose rose—the one with a succulent heart. "Jake," I said, "this ceiling is going to be better than the Sistine."

Jake laughed. "I wish I could agree," he said. "But thanks for the compliment." I started to leave, and Jake called after me, "Let's eat lunch under the towers. Sound like a plan?"

Worried that I would sound like a fool if I told him how good a plan I thought it was, I answered, "Okay with me. If you want to."

The anticipation of sharing lunch with Jake in the Tower Garden was tamping down the bad news I was holding inside me, and thinking about Jake's plan for my ceiling was crowding out the possibility of my thinking up a plan for Phase One.

Jake hopped down from the scaffold and reached for the fan. He set it down on the plank of his scaffold and tossed me the cord. "I don't suppose this will reach from here to the outlet," he said. "I better set it on the floor, and tilt it up. Next week, I'll bring an extension cord."

"The Uncles have miles of extension cords," I said. "They used to work on the towers at night. I'll bring you one."

Jake murmured thanks and turned his attention to the book of roses. He laid the glass globe on the bed and spread the photocopies out on top of the dresser. On a piece of cardboard, he measured off five inches on one side and six on the other. With a craft knife, he cut a window in the cardboard. He held the window over the copy of the rose so that the pistils and stamens were in the center—the same spot as the overhead light in the room. He traced the outline of the cardboard window right onto the photocopy and then, with a very fine pen, drew a half-inch graph on the color copy. There were ten squares in one direction and twelve in the other, just like the grid on the bedroom ceiling.

"Now, on each ceiling square, I will draw an outline of what I see in the corresponding square here," he explained. "When I'm ready to paint, I will do the same with the colors. I hope to get a good start on my drawing today," he said. He untied the bandanna from around his forehead and wiped his face. "Why don't you find those extension cords for us?" he asked.

I heard an echo of Mrs. Kaplan in that *us*, and, willing gofer that I had been just minutes ago, I went reluctantly to look for the cords. I returned to the dining room and kicked the box with the handcuffs and duct tape. What was the matter with me? Just minutes ago, I was anxious for Uncle Alex to leave so that I could be alone with Jake. Just minutes ago I was ready to fix *us* a nice picnic tray so that we could eat lunch under the towers. I seemed to like us but not *us*. Maybe Mrs. Kaplan and Nurse Louise were right. Maybe I was incorrigible after all. I kicked the box again and rattled the chain of the handcuffs. Then I remembered that the Uncles kept their extension cords in the basement.

I found yards and yards of yellow wire coiled into a nest on the floor next to the pile of wooden planks that the Uncles had used to create their workstation. I did not know that a coil of wires could be too heavy for me to lift, so I looked for a place where two lengths of cord had been joined. I found one and then another and another. I needed only one of those lengths—after all, my bedroom was not that large, and the cord would not have to reach farther than halfway across. Untangling it was not easy, for the wire was not wound neatly into a spool but in layers that crossed over and under themselves. I decided to take my time bringing *us* the extension cord, so I sat down on the pile of boards and studied the coil until I found a free end, and I began to unwind.

I remembered that when the Uncles were putting the clock face on Tower Three, they had laid the boards across the rungs so that when they stood, they could easily reach the top. My mother told me that she and Loretta Bevilaqua had sometimes climbed up to one of the platforms and would use it as a tree house of sorts until the Uncles had to move the boards to their next workstation.

I had loosened one whole length of extension cord. It was as twisted as a strand of DNA, but at least it was separated from the mass. I held one end between my thumb and forefinger and wound it around my elbow, as I had seen my uncles doing. I stood beside the pile of lumber—winding, winding—absently thinking about the planks that had once been a platform and would no longer be one . . . except . . . except . . . except, of course! The planks would again be a platform. They would be my platform. They would be my tree house of sorts. By the time I finished winding, I had a plan.

I was excited. I had a plan. I would take possession of the towers—nine points of the law—and prove they were safe at the same time.

I ran upstairs with the extension cord and quickly plugged one end to the fan and the other to the wall. Breathless with excitement, I said, "We have to talk."

Jake, who was carefully making lines on the second of the photocopies, held his pencil in midair and continued to look at the drawing. "Sure," he said. "Let's talk. What do you want to talk about?"

"Money."

"I don't have enough to talk about. End of conversation." He glanced over at the fan. "That works really well. Thanks."

"I want a refund from Camp Talequa."

He laughed. "I think your uncle and my mother already settled that between them. Tillie Kaplan does not give refunds."

"I need a refund. Really, really need it."

Putting his pencil behind his ear, he crossed his arms over his chest and said, "Margaret Rose, I really, really hate to tell you this, but the last two people to get a refund from Camp Talequa were the parents of the girl who came down with Lyme disease the second day of camp. They blamed the deer ticks in the woods near the camp even though no one had been near the woods and even though the girl's symptoms could not possibly have shown up that fast. But these were not ordinary parents. They were lawyers. Both of them. They sent Tillie a letter on cream-colored, heavy-bond stationery that was just one step short of parchment. They politely requested a refund of their full deposit. They didn't even threaten to sue—they didn't need to—their letterhead said enough. They got a check by return mail."

"You mean that lawyers can scare even Mrs. Kaplan?"

"Tillie Kaplan would rather risk bungee jumping off the Verrazano Bridge than risk a lawsuit from a husband-and-wife team of lawyers with killer stationery."

I thought, My uncles have lawyers to the left and lawyers to the right who have tasteful wooden signs that are just as lethal as any letterhead. "My situation also involves lawyers," I said, "and I need a refund."

"You may also need a lawyer to plead your case."

"How about the cash that my mother and father put in my personal Camp Talequa account, the money they left with her for my incidental needs like candy bars and postage stamps? I didn't spend any of it."

"Oh, that money! You mean your uncle didn't take it with him when he brought you back?"

"He didn't."

"I can take care of that. You won't even have to send a threatening letter."

"When?"

"Right after you tell me what you need it for."

"I've got to get supplies."

"Supplies for what?"

"For camping out."

"I thought you were finished with that for the rest of the summer."

"This is not recreational. This is business. Serious business."

"Oh," Jake said. "*Serious* business. Well, that changes everything."

Serious business. I wondered again if he was being sarcastic. "I need your attention, Jake," I said. "I need you to listen to me—really listen, really, really listen—and you'll see that what I have to say is serious enough to be a matter of life and death."

"A matter of life and death? Well now, that does sound serious."

Two sarcasms, and I was sure that he had a syndrome and that I was falling out of love. I took a deep breath. "I wouldn't ask for your help if I didn't need it."

"Do you want to discuss this over lunch?" Now all the mockery was gone from his voice. "Let me wash up," he said as he started toward the bathroom. I stood there, waiting. "Go on," he said. "I'll meet you in the Tower Garden."

"In the kitchen," I said.

"I thought we had a plan."

"I prefer the kitchen," I said.

"Whatever you prefer," he said, and waited for me to return his smile.

I did. No reason not to. I had his attention.

Even when the news was bad—as this surely was—I always got a certain shudder of excitement, which is called a *frisson*, at being the first to tell. I was embarrassed that this was so, but not so embarrassed that I did not feel my blood warm at the drama of what I had to say— and at what I guessed would be Jake's reaction to it.

I was not disappointed. He bounded up from his chair and lifted it, jammed it back down onto the floor, sat down with a thump, and pounded the table. "Who are these Philistines?"

"The neighbors. They're lawyers."

"They can't do this!"

Feeling very grown up, I replied, "Yes, they can. They can unless we stop them." I told him about my conversations with Peter Vanderwaal and Loretta Bevilaqua, and how each of them had told me that step one was to stop the demolition. "Possession is nine points of the law," I explained, "so I am going to buy the towers as Loretta said I should, and then I am going to occupy them. Will you help?"

I told Jake what I hoped to do, and we discussed it as equals. We made a list and checked it twice. After we reviewed who would do what and when, Jake said, "Sounds like a plan." And we shook hands on it.

When Jake was ready to head back to Camp Talequa, I walked out to the alley with him. He looked up at Tower Two. "Are you sure you want to do this?" he asked.

I nodded.

"Are you scared?"

I nodded again.

"Good," he said. "If you're scared, you won't get careless."

nineteen

I got through dinner without mentioning the towers even once, and afterward Uncle Alex and I took Tartufo for his walk. "Tartufo likes to walk at night," he said. "In Italy where he was born, they train truffle dogs mostly at night because the *tartufai,* the truffle hunters, like to keep their best locations secret. People have been known to kidnap prize truffle dogs. Truffle hunting is a very competitive business. The season is short, and the rewards are high. There is safety in secrets."

"What if Tartufo never finds any truffles, Uncle?"

"I don't care. He keeps me doing something from within myself for the sake of something that is not. Tartufo is good company."

"Uncle Morris doesn't think so."

"Yes, he does. That's his secret, *édes* Margitkám. We'll let him keep it."

"Doing something from within yourself for something that is not—is that why you built the towers?"

"Probably. They kept Morris and me going through

some bad times. It was good having something that was common to both of us and was its own thing besides. Other people have children they raise. The children are from both parents, but also someone in their own right. They are good company while you have them, but you have to let them go."

"Like the towers, Uncle? Is that why you don't care that the towers are coming down?"

Uncle Alex stopped short, but Tartufo kept going, tugging on the leash. Without looking at me, he resumed walking. "So you know."

"Yes, I know."

"I guess I should be relieved. Neither Morris nor I could bring ourselves to tell you."

"Because you really do care."

"Of course we care. But it's like having kids or like having Tartufo. Having had them is more important than keeping them. Can you understand that, *édes* Margitkám?"

"Not really."

"Maybe it will take a few more years."

"A few more years? I thought they were going to start next week."

"I mean, a few more years for you to understand that ''Tis better to have loved and lost than never to have loved at all.'"

"What's that?"

"Tennyson."

"Was he an artist?"

"No. A poet who lost a dear friend." I reached over for Uncle's hand. "Yeah," he said, lifting my hand to his lips and kissing my fingertips. "Friends, sisters, towers. Loved and lost. There's nothing more to say."

When we returned to the house, Uncle Alex said to Uncle Morris, "She knows."

"You told her?"

"I did not."

"Then how does she know?"

I hated having people talk about me in the third person as if I weren't there. "Why don't you ask me?"

"So?" Uncle Morris asked. "You found out how?"

By careful editing, leaving out as much as I put in, I told them how I had found out. I worried whether not telling them my plans was a lie and decided that it wasn't. It was a secret. And hadn't Uncle just said that there is safety in secrets? Feeling relieved about telling the truth but not the whole truth, I asked my uncles if they would sell me the towers for a dollar a piece. (As part of our afternoon planning, Jake had given me a cash advance on the refund I was due from Talequa.)

"Why do you want them, Margitkám? You will have

the house. It's in our will that you will inherit the
house. The towers? They are not worth anything at all.
They are what we call in business a liability."

"Not to me. I want to say they're mine even if it is
only for a little while. Like having children."

Uncle Alex, who caught the reference and was
touched by it, said, "Morris, the child wants them. Give
them to her."

"No," I insisted. "I must buy them. I have the
money."

"All right," he said. Then, turning to his brother, he
said, "Alex, you write up a paper."

"And we'll get it notarized."

"Notarized? Where did you learn of such things?"

I did my best imitation of the Old World shrug.
"Sixth grade."

The following morning my uncles and I made a trip to
the bank where they normally did their Time Zone
business. Mr. McDowell, their loan officer, made out an
official bill of sale. Before I turned over my three dollars
to complete the sale, Mr. McDowell asked my uncles,
"Does this niece of yours realize that if anyone gets
hurt as a result of something falling from them or if
anyone falls off of them, she can be sued?"

I truly hated being talked about as if I weren't there.

I said, "We have a fence and a vicious dog to keep them out. If they get in, they'll be trespassing."

Mr. McDowell still wouldn't talk to me. "Does your niece know that the towers have been condemned?"

"Condemned?" I asked. "Condemned to die like someone guilty of a crime?"

That got his attention, and at last he addressed me. "In the case of a building, it means unfit for use by official order."

"Unfit for use! How stupid! The towers have no use. My mother says that they don't need to be useful. She says that they are superfluous and that is their power because, without them, our world would be less beautiful and a lot less fun."

Mr. McDowell said, "She's a sassy one, isn't she?"

"She?" Uncle Alex asked. "You must not mean our Margaret Rose. Our Margaret Rose isn't sassy. She's incorrigible."

Mr. McDowell cleared his throat and notarized the bill of sale.

twenty

For the next five days, between the time that Uncle Alex left for the Time Zone and the time Uncle Morris returned, I laid in supplies. I already had a rain poncho, a sleeping bag, sunblock, and mosquito repellent among the stuff that I had brought back from Talequa.

I bought quantities of bottled water, trail mix, beef jerky, and towelettes. These items required multiple trips by bus to various distant strip malls so that I could avoid those that were near Schuyler Place or my family home because I didn't want anyone who knew me to spot me. And, of course, I stayed clear of the Fivemile Creek Mall. I bought a little bit at a time so that I could find places to stash things. Every time I went out, I bought a pound of cottage cheese, ate some, dumped the rest, washed the container, and stashed it in my bottom dresser drawer.

I also made many important long-distance phone calls.

I called Loretta Bevilaqua at work and got her *administray assist,* who insisted that Ms. Bevilaqua could not come to the phone, but I was free to leave a message either with him or on voice mail.

"When will she get it?" I asked.

"When she checks her messages."

"Can I tell her not to call me during certain hours?"

"You certainly may, but, of course, that could delay her response."

I chose voice mail. I said that I now owned *them*. I said that *they* cost three dollars. And that *it* was notarized, but I didn't ask for a return call.

I always had better luck reaching Peter Vanderwaal. Either a polite female voice said, "Sheboygan Art Center," and then connected me directly to Peter, or Peter himself answered. He reported that he was making progress on getting the CPC organized, but it was taking a lot longer than he had thought it would. "At my own expense, I am sending letters out by Federal Express with prepaid return envelopes, and you have no idea—I certainly didn't—how expensive that has turned out to be. So far I have received only three of them back. When I call to remind them, they don't call back."

I sympathized with him and told him the difficulties I was having in reaching Loretta. Peter said, "I thought she would return calls directly."

"Why did you think that?"

"Because she is a truly busy person. Truly busy

people don't dillydally. They are decisive and they return phone calls. It's those of lesser importance who have to impress you with how busy they are and how they can't get around to your request."

"But she has an administray assist."

"Darling," Peter said, "you are sunk unless you can find some way to get around her."

"Him."

"Worse," Peter said. "When the administrative assistant is a male, he is hell-bent on proving how important he is, so he works overtime protecting his boss from the people she has to do business with. Tell me, don't you have any way to get around him?"

I said that I had a home number, but when Loretta's business hours were over and the administray assist was off duty, my uncles were home, and I didn't want to make or receive calls then. And that's when Peter Vanderwaal volunteered to be my go-between. "Give me that number, and I'll be your administrative assistant, darling, and you can just go about your business of stopping the demolition." I thanked him, and he said, "Nothing to it. I'm coming home this weekend to light a fire under a few art professors at Clarion State University. They should be mounting the barricades instead of sitting on their writing hands. I hope to shame them into becoming active."

"Will I see you?" I asked.

"You tell me when to come, and we'll have a secret visit in the Tower Garden. You'll recognize me even though I don't look at all like that picture in my mother's office. I probably don't look like anyone you've ever seen. I have a diamond stud in my left ear; I always wear a bow tie; and I shave my head. But, trust me, you'll find me adorable."

I could hardly wait.

He was pinker and rounder than I had pictured him in my mind, but he was everything else I had hoped he would be. When he said *we*—as in "We ought to go to Summit Street and get a *latte*"—that *we* meant him, Peter, and me, Margaret, and the *latte* meant a cup of coffee with a lot of steamy milk in it served in a special glass with a metal holder.

As we sat at the small round table that was outside the restaurant, I put my elbows on the table, leaned forward, and stared deeply into Peter's eyes. He was so fascinating. "How is your father's dialysis?" I asked.

"Oh, he's all right. It sure keeps Mother busy, and that's good."

"Why is that good?"

"What with all the care she has to give Dad, I don't think she wants grandchildren at the moment, so she doesn't keep asking me when I'm going to get married. Mothers are so needy."

I let my wrist go limp as I dangled my *latte* spoon in my right hand. "You don't care for children?"

"I can stand a few of them as individuals, but, God forgive me, not in groups."

I stirred my drink and took a sip and, in my best movie-star manner, looked at Peter over the rim of my glass before putting it down. "That's fascinating. I thought the very same thing after my experience with Talequa."

"Talequa? What's a Talequa?"

"It's a summer camp where I was being warehoused."

"Well," Peter said, "I had a summer camp experience once. Day camp. Two weeks. It was not pleasant, but then, neither was I."

"Oh!" I said, marveling at how much we had in common. "I was called incorrigible."

"How did you escape?"

"Uncle Alex rescued me."

"Well, Margaret Rose, you must regard all of life's experiences as corners in the maze of life. Round the corner or bump into it. It's all part of getting there."

"Getting where?"

"To being grown up."

"Is being grown up worth it?"

"You betcha."

"Why?"

"Because grown-ups get to make all the movies, get to lead all the orchestras, and get to get their ears pierced without asking permission."

We laughed, and I decided that we were the two most sophisticated people drinking *lattes* at a little round table on the pedestrian mall in all of Epiphany and possibly France. "Has Loretta told you what she has planned to do to save the towers?"

"No. She's a lawyer, you know. You can't wedge a toothpick between her lips if her lips are sealed. She just keeps telling me that I am Phase Two. As if repetition is the mother of intervention."

"She keeps telling me that I am Phase One."

"And she is Phase Three. And the only hint she will give me is that her famous Phase Three has something to do with Infinitel, and that she has to make a presentation to the board of directors. Poor thing. I, too, have a board of directors. The funny thing is that they love me so much they expect me to *tell* them what I want, and then they expect me to ask their permission to do it. Have you ever had to deal with a board?"

"Yes," I replied, "the board of education. And from what I read in the papers, they can't agree on anything except how many days we are to spend in school." What I was saying was not exactly true because at that point in my life, I never read the paper. (If I had, I would have had at least a hint that the towers were coming down.)

Peter looked at his watch, a huge thing as big as a sundial with enough bells and whistles to run a railroad. "I have an appointment with two professors from the Art Department and two from the History Department. I hope to get their signatures on the CPC petition today so that I can get it into my mother's hands. She's promised to sneak it on to the city council agenda when they meet next time. What time did you say your uncles get home?"

"On Saturdays, they both stay until closing. They won't be getting home until about ten."

"Good," Peter said. "I'll be bringing by four professors—two from art and two from history— later this afternoon. I want to show them what a treasure we have here in Old Town."

"That will be fine," I said. "You have my permission."

Peter, who had just raised his arm toward the waitress to signal for the check, let his hand go limp. "Permission?" he asked.

"Yes. If I didn't give my permission, they would be trespassing. I own the towers now. I bought them this past week. I have the bill of sale in my underwear drawer. It's notarized."

"You own the towers?"

"Yes. Loretta insisted that I buy them."

"She did, did she? I wish she had asked me to buy them."

"Why?"

"I would have loved to own them. I would be their proud possessor—even if only for a little while. Do you think that's just too, too romantic?"

I replied, "'Tis better to have loved and lost than never to have loved at all.'"

"Ah, yes! Tennyson," he said. He got a faraway look in his eyes, and then he snapped back to attention. "In the meantime, you have Phase One to carry out: Stop them. And I have Phase Two: Stall them. Stop and Stall. Has a good ring to it." The waitress came and gave Peter the check. He paid with cash, piling the bills on top of the tab. "Margaret Rose, my dear, when I was growing up on Schuyler Place, I never once thought that there would come a day when I would spend three dollars for a cup of coffee—and enjoy it! But then, I never knew that the daughter of my chum Naomi Landau would provide me with such charming company. Now I'm off to meet the supremes of academe."

"Are they rainmakers?"

"They think they are, but frankly, my dear, all four of them together couldn't fill a *latte* cup with piss."

twenty-one

On the Tuesday evening before Jake's next visit, the Uncles walked around their garden. Tartufo ran figure eights around the base of Towers One and Two. Uncle Alex held his hands behind his back and scanned the towers top to bottom. "On Thursday," he said, "the workmen will come to wrap the towers in netting to keep loosened pieces from falling on someone. This old Tower Garden will become a hard-hat area."

Uncle Morris examined his pepper plants. "Some of these will rot," he said. "Let them." Then he had a second thought. "Tell Jake to help himself to whatever he wants. He can take some back to Talequa."

"You can tell him yourself, Uncle. He'll be here early in the morning."

"No, I'll be at the mall. The Mall Association decided to have a Bastille Day Blowout. Uncle Alex and I will both work both shifts. We'll be gone all day Wednesday to prepare and all day Thursday, hopefully to sell."

Uncle Alex told me that he was counting on me to take care of Tartufo both days.

That meant that Jake and I would have all day to carry out our plans instead of having to crowd the work into the hours between the time Uncle Alex left and Uncle Morris came home.

"*Jaj, Istenem!*" Uncle Morris said. "Twelve hours of being cooped up in the Time Zone with my brother makes me wish I was an only child. By the second day, I fear that I may arrange it."

When Jake arrived, we wasted no time in putting our plan into action.

We had chosen Tower Two, and we had chosen a height that was above the rooftops but where the tower was still wide enough for a platform that would allow enough space to store all of my supplies and still give me room to sit or lie down.

Jake climbed up first and measured the span between the uprights. Then together we went to the basement to choose boards that were long enough to rest easily on the rungs. There were not enough of them, so we hurried to the lumber store and had planks cut to the correct lengths.

When we returned with the lumber, Tartufo would not let me out of his sight. He circled my legs, as twitchy as an ADD, an Attention Deficit Dog.

After assembling all the boards, we constructed a

platform by lifting planks from my bedroom window to the rungs of Tower Two that were just above the height of the window. From inside the room, I pushed them through the open window at an angle that allowed Jake to reach down, grab them, and lift them into place. After two were down, he lashed them to each other and to the horizontal rungs. The knots—hitch knots—tightened when pulled.

"Impressed?" he asked.

"Very."

"I was a Boy Scout. Surprised?"

"Very."

When the last of the boards was in place and tied down, Jake bounced up and down a few times and declared, "Sturdy enough for one twelve-year-old and her supplies." My living space would be a square platform, four feet on a side.

Finally, we laid a wide board to reach from the platform to the open bedroom window to use as a gangplank. It rested at a steep angle, which made navigating dangerous, but by being cautious and by not hurrying, we managed to transfer all my accumulated supplies without a single slip.

We worked from a list I had prepared: a poncho for rain; an umbrella for sun; water (lots of water); crackers, beef jerky, and trail mix; a Walkman; three books from my summer reading list; my documents of ownership in a gallon-size Ziploc plastic bag; a flashlight; and a stack of cottage cheese containers with lids.

Without a word, Jake picked up the stack of cottage cheese containers and carried it down the plank, across the bedroom, down the stairs, and into the kitchen, where he deposited it in the trash on his way to his truck, which was parked in the alley. I waited on the platform, wondering.

Jake returned with two things: a chemical toilet and a tarpaulin that he used to cover furniture and floors when he was painting. "I'll drape this over three sides of the platform. I'll leave the side next to the house open. That should give you enough privacy for when you use this," he said, pointing to the chemical toilet. "Tillie has an inventory of these things for camping trips at Talequa. I borrowed one."

I was too embarrassed to say something and too grateful not to. I said, *"Köszönöm,"* a simple "thank you" in Hungarian, and he understood.

"I told you I was once a Boy Scout. We were trained to help ladies in distress."

It was late afternoon when we finished. Jake did some work on his drawing of the rose as I warmed up leftovers for our supper. We had little to say to each other as we ate, but Tartufo made up for our quiet. He whimpered. He pranced around my legs, his nails clattering on the kitchen linoleum like hail hitting a tin roof. He was demanding more attention than I had time or patience for. I knew I had to give him a good long walk. I invited Jake to come along. "Sure," he said, lighting a cigar on his way out. He took the leash from me as soon as we were out the door.

"Let me," I said. "It will be our last walk for a while." Jake turned the leash back over to me. I was relieved to have something to do that kept me from linking arms with him.

We walked down one side of Schuyler Place, and as we passed number 17, I told him about my failure as a starter baby-sitter. We walked back on the other side of the street. Jake stopped at the same spot as I had the week before. He gazed over the rooftops at Tower Two. Some of the glass pendants caught tiny pinpoints of light from the streetlamp, and the slight breeze set some of them to trembling like wind chimes. Jake shook his head. "How could anyone—*anyone*—believe that taking those towers down would improve the neighborhood?"

"Some of us don't."

"And at the moment, Margaret Rose Kane, we are the sum of the some." And with that, he swept me up into his arms and carried me across the street. It would have been as romantic as a groom carrying a bride across a threshold if Tartufo had not gone wild and nipped at Jake's heels all the way.

When we returned to the platform, we again checked the supplies against my list. Tartufo wailed so long and loud that Jake slammed the bedroom window down onto the plank that was resting on the sill. He succeeded in muffling the sound slightly. At last he asked, "Are you ready?" My throat was too dry to answer, so I nodded yes. I put the heavy athletic sock from my uncles' box on my right foot, and folded down the cuff once and then again. Jake looked at me for a final okay before locking one hoop of the cuffs to my ankle and the other to the vertical post of Tower Two.

He pocketed the key and climbed back down the plank and through the bedroom window. Before he could pull the plank back through, Tartufo jumped, and in one giant leap he landed on the plank on three of his four feet. He did not take his eyes off me as he scratched and scrambled and reassembled his hindquarters. All of my outer self was frozen with fear, but my stomach roiled like a tsunami and my heart pounded like surf erupting on shore. At last Tartufo managed to get all four paws on the plank and made his way grandly—head held high—onto the platform by my side.

"Get back here," Jake yelled.

"Must he?" I asked.

"Of course he must. You can't keep him up there."

"Why not?"

"For one thing, Tartufo can't use a cottage cheese container or a chemical toilet."

"How are you going to get him back?"

"I'll climb back up there, get behind him, and shove."

"What if he slides off the plank and falls?"

"What if I do?"

"You won't."

"Neither will he."

"Uncle Alex asked me to take care of him."

"He's going to be no end of trouble."

"But he'll also be good company."

Jake was tired. He had no energy left to convince me, so he shrugged and pulled the plank through the bedroom window. "That dog is going to be no end of trouble," he repeated, half to himself, half to the almost-rose ceiling. He slammed the window shut, locked it from the inside, and left.

I stood upright, high up in the night sky, feeling as if the mild summer breeze could pass through my ribs as easily as it did the ribs of Tower Two. I reached over to Tartufo. "Well, we've done it," I said. At that moment I could not have said whether *done it* meant that I was where I wanted to be or that I had alienated the last person in the world that I wanted to.

 Nine Points

twenty-two

It was a long night.

How could I have known how much having a leg fastened to the tower would cramp my sleeping style? How could I have known that I had a sleeping style? Tartufo's insistence on keeping close company didn't help either. Around ten thirty, I heard my uncles' muffled voices as they entered the darkened house. I'm sure they saw my closed bedroom door and decided not to disturb me. I heard Uncle Alex calling for Tartufo.

In the dim light from the streetlamp, I saw Tartufo lift his head. His ears perked up. I held my breath. I did not want to be discovered until it was too late for them to do anything about it. "Shush," I whispered. Then, as I had often heard Uncle Alex do, I spoke to him in his native language, using the only word I knew. *"Capisci?"* The calling stopped. Uncle Alex must have gone to bed thinking that Tartufo was with me behind the closed door of my bedroom. "It's all right," I whispered. "It's all right," I repeated. Tartufo wagged his tail and laid his head in the narrow parting of his front paws.

• • •

Even though I was certain that I had not slept a wink all night, I later reasoned that I must have. Otherwise, why would I remember being awakened by the sound of men's voices? The first thing I saw was Tartufo, up on all fours, standing at attention, waiting for instructions to bark or not to. I held my finger over my lips, and Tartufo sat down, his ears forward. What a good dog he was. How could Jake have said that he would be no end of trouble? He was a comfort and a companion.

I lifted a corner of the tarp and saw three men standing outside the fence, resting their forearms on its top rail. They seemed to be studying the towers. The morning breeze had shifted, and their conversation came to me in puffs of sound.

"... never seen nothing like this ..."

"Why ... want to take them down?"

"... not safe ..."

"... neighborhood look bad ..."

"... look good to me ..."

The men took rolls of yellow tape out of the back of their truck, opened the back gate, and came inside the yard. They started stretching the tape from post to post along the fence. It looked like the CRIME-SCENE tape I had seen on the TV news. I was too far away to read what it said, but I believed that what these men were about to do was a crime, and any tape that said so was perfectly suitable. (I later learned that it said CAUTION.)

Tartufo was quiet until the man who had been sitting in the driver's seat of the truck came into the yard. And then he began to bark. Tarfufo knew a villain when he saw one. He got louder and louder and more and more insistent. The men holding the rolls of yellow plastic tape began to back away. In another minute, Uncle Alex, in bare feet and a short terry-cloth robe, came to the back door. Uncle Morris, similarly dressed, followed. Uncle Morris's comb-over stood up like a cockscomb. The two of them shielded their eyes with their hands and focused on the source of Tartufo's barking.

I laughed with relief. My secret was out. My plan was under way.

"Hi," I called down.

"What are you doing up there, Margitkám?"

"Taking possession," I answered. "Possession is nine points of the law."

"Is Tartufo all right?" Uncle Alex asked.

"See for yourself," I answered. "He's been up here with me all night." I beckoned Tartufo to come to the edge of the platform to show Uncle what fine shape he was in.

The fat driver of the truck came all the way into the

yard and stood at the bottom of the back steps in front of the Uncles. He yelled up at me, "You can come down now, young lady."

"I can't," I answered.

"Don't tell me you can't."

"See for yourself," I said, standing up awkwardly. "I am tethered," I yelled, stretching my leg so that he could see the length of chain.

"You come down this minute," the fat man called. "We have a job to do."

"So do I."

"And what is that, young lady?"

"To stop you."

"Well, I'm afraid you won't be able to do that. I have an order from City Hall to take these towers down."

"And I have possession," I said. "Possession is nine points of the law. As soon as you touch these towers, you are trespassing."

The Uncles looked at each other and smiled, and in a gesture of harmony I had never before witnessed, they hugged each other and laughed out loud. "We've got to get to work now," Uncle Morris said.

Uncle Alex asked, "Do you have something to eat up there?"

"I do."

"Lunch?"

"Lunch, too."

"Good," he said. "We'll stop back before we leave for the day in case there's anything you need." With a wave that was very close to being a salute, they went back inside the house.

Tartufo barked.

After the tape was stretched all around the fence, one of the men drove tall stakes into the earth around the path that separated the roses and peppers garden from the towers. A second man stretched the yellow tape from stake to stake, and the third fastened triangular red flags on to the yellow tape. They did not seem to be in a hurry, and after they finished hanging the flags, they congregated in the far corner of the yard. They folded their arms across their chests and said nothing, but they smiled as they studied the towers and talked among themselves.

The foreman, whose name I soon learned was Tony, walked back to his truck and took a clipboard from the seat and a can of Coke from the dashboard. He returned to Tower Two, pulled a page from the clipboard, and waved it in the air. "I have papers from City Hall," he said.

"I have papers too," I said, leaning over to reach the plastic bag containing my proof of ownership. "I own these towers, and I forbid you to set foot on them. If you try, I'll have you arrested for trespassing."

Tony took a long swig from the can of Coke, crushed the can in one hand, and tossed it on the ground.

"Pick that up," I said, "or I'll have you arrested for littering as well as trespassing."

"Come down and make me."

"Ha! Nice try." I thrust my manacled foot out as far as the chain would allow. "Sorry," I said, "but I already told you, I am tethered."

"Who are you, anyway?"

"I am Margaret Rose, and this is Tartufo, and we belong here, and you don't."

"I have a court order," he said. He took a deep breath. "These towers are coming down, young lady, right after you do."

"Sorry," I said.

"You will be coming down, little girl, if we have to personally climb up there with an acetylene torch and burn that thing off your leg." He paused just a minute and added, "Now, what say you just tell us where the key is, and we'll have you down here in a minute."

It was probably his saying "if *we* have to" and "just tell *us*" that got to me. I said, "I prefer not to."

A stifled laugh came from the direction of the three

helpers. For a man with a dirigible for a stomach, Tony managed to turn toward them real fast, and the men managed to turn their backs on him just as fast. They started straightening stakes that did not need straightening and tightening tape that didn't need tightening. Tony decided to take a kinder, gentler approach. "Who put you up there, little girl?" he asked.

"I am here of my own free will."

"What about that dog?"

"He volunteered. As a matter of fact, he insisted."

"Yeah?" he said. "We'll see about that." He called to the three men, "C'mon guys. We've got work to do elsewhere." He paused by the gate and said, "I'll be back."

"Don't hurry on my account," I replied.

As he turned to leave, I heard him say to the other men, "That cocky little she-brat is gonna pay."

I watched one of the three men pick up the bent Coke can and toss it over the back fence. I heard it hit the floor of the truck bed and watched the man who threw it look up at me, smile, and give me a thumbs-up.

For many reasons—not the least of which was my need to take care of certain body functions—I was happy to see them go. I pulled the flap of tarp back down. The only side that was left open was the side facing the house. I tried to think of myself as sitting on a howdah until Tartufo came over and sat in front of me. He made me so self-conscious that my normal morning call of nature went unanswered. I was numb. I couldn't go. "Move," I said to Tartufo. "Go," I urged. "Go away," I scolded. I knew that *capisci* did not mean what I needed it to mean, but it was the only word I knew in his native language, and I thought it sounded like what I needed to do. Onomatopoeia. *"Capisci!"* I said, and I added, *"Capisco!"*—with emphasis on the second syllable. But Tartufo did not move. He continued to stare. I told myself that Tartufo was only a dog, only a dog, only a dog. When I realized that even though he was only a dog, he would have the same need I had, my worries shifted from me to him, and I was able to answer nature's call.

Dressed now and ready for work, my uncles came into the yard and called up to me. I lifted the tarp and asked them what I could do about Tartufo.

Uncle Alex had a quick answer. "Let him go against the vertical pole. Then step back as far as you can. I'll hose it down."

"Simple," I said, relieved. "Thanks."

Uncle Morris helped by turning the water on and off after Uncle Alex had carefully aimed the jet to the exact place where Tartufo went.

• • •

When Tony's truck returned, it was leading a caravan. A fire engine followed him, and a white Animal Control van from the Society for the Prevention of Cruelty to Animals followed the fire engine. Tartufo was to be rescued. Animals, it seemed, had rights that overruled the nine-points rule; and that is when Jake's prediction that Tartufo was going to be *no end of trouble* came true.

The fire truck pulled up to the front of 19 Schuyler Place and ran its long ladder against the front of the house. A fireman and the animal control person climbed across the roof, lifted themselves up the rungs of the towers to my platform, and took Tartufo, who barked and fought. But these men were experienced at handling mad dogs, and his nipping and yipping hardly slowed them down. I screamed and yelled and told them they had no right, but they paid no attention to me, either. They didn't even answer me until I asked where they were taking him, and they said, "The county pound." They put him in the white van, and even after I heard the doors close, I could hear him whining. It was pitiful.

Tony came into the yard and picked up the garden hose that Uncle Alex had left lying on the ground. He called to one of his assistants to turn it on. "Full force!" he commanded.

The man, the one who had given me a thumbs-up,

said, "Not a good idea, Tony. You'll make her slippery."

"And I'll also make her wet. Turn it on, I tell you."

The man walked away. Swearing and cursing me, the men, the day—everything!—Tony walked over to the spigot and turned it on. He adjusted the nozzle to jet stream and aimed. I dropped the tarp, but it was no use. The force of the jet lifted it as easily as a flamenco dancer's petticoats.

I grabbed the plastic bag of my ownership papers and wrapped it in my poncho. I watched my crackers, beef jerky, and trail mix become soup, and my Walkman, flashlight, and three summer-reading-list books get ruined. But my double-wrapped documents stayed dry. By standing with my back to the spray, I managed to open my umbrella. I used it like a shield, but Tony managed to drag the hose around so that he took steady aim at the inside of the umbrella until it turned inside out and became useless. Then he aimed at my face. I closed my eyes and tried to shield my face with my arms, but I lost my balance and fell. Fell in such an awkward position with my shackled leg twisted behind me that I could not maneuver, and I had to endure the full force of the jet stream with my eyes closed and my hands shielding my face as best they could.

While I was trying to keep from drowning, I did not

see or hear—how could I possibly have seen or heard anything?—the firemen entering the Tower Garden from the alley. I did not know they were there until I heard a fireman yelling, "What in hell do you think you are doing?"

And then the water suddenly stopped.

I had only a brief minute of believing I was saved, for in the time it took for the fireman to reach the spigot, another had scaled the tower and was standing behind me. I was twisted into the place where I had fallen. I could not see him, but I heard him say, "Stay calm, miss. I won't hurt you."

From my awkward position, I could see a second fireman making his way up the rungs of the tower. Not certain if the platform could hold his weight as well as mine, he called to the men below and told them to spread a net. Still invisible to me, I heard the man behind me say, "It's okay. It'll hold." And then he gently locked my arms behind me and waited until the second man reached the rungs just below my platform.

He had a ring of keys. One by one, he tried them on the cuffs. On the fourth try he succeeded, and he called down to the men waiting at the foot of the ladder, "Got it!"

Wet and humiliated, I was slung over the fireman's shoulder and carried down.

Tony looked on with satisfaction.

The three workmen, with sympathy.

twenty-three

Without sirens blaring or lights flashing, I was taken to the juvenile detention center in a police car. I was delivered to a large woman who sat behind a large desk on the third floor. She had a barrel-shaped neck that sat on shoulders broad enough to balance epaulets as wide as cookie spatulas. She smiled when she saw me. Unlike Mrs. Kaplan's, her smile was not appliquéd but included her eyes, her mouth, and the laugh lines that connected them. She smiled when she was amused. I obviously amused her, which did not amuse me.

"Aren't I allowed one phone call?" I asked.

She laughed. "Been watching a lot of TV?"

"That's not an answer," I replied. "Can I or can I not make a phone call?"

She slid the phone across her desk. "Be my guest."

"I would like a little privacy," I said.

She looked around the room. "I say that to myself— oh, about three, maybe four times a day. Sorry, but this is the only phone we have available for our criminals."

"I am not a criminal. I am here for protective custody. They didn't even put on the sirens when they brought me in."

She laughed again. "That in itself should be considered criminal." She pointed her chin toward the phone. "Dial 9 for an outside line."

"I've done that before," I said.

"Have you also reversed charges to make a long-distance call?"

"Yes, I have. But what do I do if they won't accept the charges?"

"Then, sweetie, you hang up and try a different friend."

To my great relief, Jake did pick up the phone, and without hesitation, he accepted the charges.

"I'm in jail," I said.

"Who is this?"

"I'm who the operator said I am. I am Margaret Rose Kane."

"Oh, *that* Margaret Rose Kane," he said, laughing nervously. "What happened?"

I told him about the SPCA and the water hose. He said nothing. The silence on his end of the line was aggravating me. "I'm in jail!" I yelled.

"Have they stopped the demolition?"

"Didn't you hear me? I'm in jail." He was really aggravating me.

"I heard you."

"I'm in jail, and Tartufo's been taken to the pound."

"Yes, but have they stopped the demolition?"

Really, really aggravating.

"How should I know? I'm in protective custody."

"Are you behind bars?"

"Might as well be. I'm in a room with an ugly steel door painted gray with one little window that has chicken wire pressed into it."

"Can you do something that will make them keep you overnight?"

"Like what?"

"Oh, I don't know. Cry or write dirty words on the walls."

"I could write the worst words in the world, and they wouldn't notice because . . . because . . . Jake, are you listening to me?"

"Yeah, I'm listening. You were saying . . . what were you saying?"

"I was saying, I can't write dirty words on the walls because they wouldn't even notice because, Jake, *they're already there*. All of them. Spelled out in capital letters."

"All right, all right. Maybe that wasn't such a good

idea. But listen, Margaret. We have to stop them at least one more day. Are you listening to me?"

"Better than you listened to me."

"What did I say?"

"What is this, Jake, a comprehension exam?"

"No. Not an exam. But a required course. There's only one more day till the weekend, and city employees never work on weekends. By Monday, Loretta Bevilaqua and Peter Vanderwaal will have their petitions ready."

"What if they euthanize Tartufo?"

"Ah, yes! Tartufo," he said. "I told you that dog would—" Then he stopped abruptly. "Where are your uncles?"

"At the mall. It's the Bastille Day Blowout. Remember?"

"I guess I'll have to call them. Once they find out where you and Tartufo are, I know they'll rescue you. Too bad."

"Too bad?" I yelled. "Did I hear you say *Too bad*?"

"Yeah. I guess I better call your uncles."

"That *is* too bad."

"Yeah. Are you sure you can't do something to make them keep you overnight? I've got plans—"

"Jacob?"

"What now?"

"Good-bye."

I hung up.

I had wasted my one phone call. Nothing was settled. I didn't know if I would get out of jail or if Tartufo would get out of the pound or if the demolition would stop.

Being a juvenile held in protective custody was making it very difficult to carry out Phase One, and even though he was an adult and had a credit card and a driver's license, my co-conspirator, Jacob Kaplan, was not helping.

As soon as he got Jake's call, Uncle Alex left the Time Zone and hailed a cab to take him to the animal pound. Uncle Morris stayed at the mall only long enough to reach Dennis the Tattoo and Helga the Reliable to take their places at the Bastille Day Blowout. Then he drove to the Clarion County Behavioral Center to rescue me.

The lady with the epaulets was reluctant to release me into Uncle Morris's care. She wanted to know why, if he was my guardian, he had been so negligent that I had been able to slip out of the house and climb the tower.

Uncle Morris's tactics in dealing with the lady with the epaulets was exactly the opposite of those that Uncle Alex had taken with Mrs. Kaplan. He humbled himself. He wrinkled his brow. He wrung his hands, and he oiled his Hungarian accent to something between mayonnaise and margarine as he explained the situation. He explained that he had left for work early that morning because of the Bastille Day Blowout at the mall, and that his brother did not mention to him that their niece was up in the tower when he left.

Nothing he said was untrue. He *had* left for work early. But so had Alex. And, of course, there had been no need for Alex to mention that I was up in the tower because he had seen it for himself.

"Where are this child's parents?"

"On a mission in South America."

"A mission in South America?"

"Yes. They have gone to Peru for four weeks."

"What kind of a mission?"

"In the Andes."

"A rescue mission?"

"I'm sure you'll read about it in the papers when they return."

"I'm going to let you take the child home with you, Mr. Rose, but you must promise me that you'll watch her."

"Like Mary Poppins I'll watch her."

"I'm warning you: If I find out that you have put that child's life in jeopardy, it's going to take an appeal to the supreme court of the United States of America to keep yourself out of jail."

"I promise that won't happen."

She pushed some papers forward and indicated that Uncle was to sign them. He did. "Thank you," he said. "Thank you very much. *Köszönöm szépen.*"

She answered, *"Nagyon szivesen."* They exchanged smiles: his, knowing; hers, more so.

Uncle Morris now had one rescue. Uncle Alex had one. I had a headache.

Back Inside the Crypto-Cabin

twenty-four

All the way back to Talequa, Jake had a worried mind. Later he told me that he had felt uneasy about leaving me high, dry, and alone on Tower Two. He was upset with himself for not having a backup plan. Hadn't Alex said that everyone should always have a backup? He knew that he should not have left without one.

It was late when he opened the door to his cabin. He found a Post-it on his coffeepot. It was from his mother. Hummingbird cabin needed new lightbulbs. He checked the time. Not quite midnight, still Wednesday, still his day off. But it was well past lights-out for the Hummingbirds, so they were already in the dark. They would see daylight before they needed new bulbs. He crumpled the note and threw it in the corner trash.

He brewed a fresh pot of coffee and sat in his chair and thought about the towers. It was funny how important they had become to him. He would not even have known that they existed if his mother had not called Uncle Alex that Sunday that I preferred not to go tubing on the lake.

—that Sunday

About an hour after the bus left, Mrs. Kaplan came into Meadowlark, carrying a plate of cookies and a container of milk. "Come, Margaret," she said. "Come sit here so that we can have a little chat." She placed the plate of cookies between us. "Help yourself," she said.

I took a cookie, said thank you, and took a bite. She smiled and waited for me to swallow. I took a second bite. She allowed me to chew a little before she said, "Today, Margaret, we hear that you preferred not to go tubing on the lake." I nodded. "As a result, Margaret, we hear that you kept an entire bus full of girls waiting while you took time to decide that you preferred not to go. Is that not so?"

"Not quite," I replied.

"Can you tell us what you mean by *not quite?*"

"Sure," I said. Mrs. Kaplan waited. "I did not hold up the bus while I made up my mind. I had made up my mind the night before. It was Gloria who held it up."

"Now, Margaret, you don't mean to tell us that Gloria would keep a busload of girls waiting? Gloria knew how eager everyone was to go tubing on the lake. Everyone but you, Margaret."

I asked, "Is that milk for me, Mrs. Kaplan?"

"Yes, it is," she replied, handing it over.

It was hot, and I was thirsty, and I could hear myself making *glug-glug* sounds. I said, "So much better than that powdered stuff you give us in the mess hall."

"The powdered milk keeps better," Mrs. Kaplan said.

"And is a lot cheaper," I replied.

"Margaret!" Mrs. Kaplan said. "Margaret?" she said softer.

"Yes, Mrs. Kaplan."

"You haven't answered our question."

"I'm afraid I didn't hear a question, Mrs. Kaplan. Would you mind repeating it?"

"You knew that everyone was eager to go tubing."

"And?"

"And you knew that Gloria would have to come to Meadowlark to get you."

"And?"

"So why do you tell us that Gloria—not you—held up the bus?"

"Because I told Gloria last night that I would not be going tubing on the lake."

"Gloria would not have held up the bus if you had told her. She is one of our finest counselors. She has seniority among all of our counselors."

"She must have selective hearing loss. It's a medical condition of seniors."

"Gloria is twenty-two years old. She's not even old enough to be your mother."

"Then she must have selective *listening.*" I paused a minute. "This morning I told three of the Alums"—here I counted on my fingers—"Alicia Silver, Ashley Schwartz, and Blair Patayani, to remind her."

"And no one heard you?"

"I guess not."

"Do you want me to believe that these girls also have selective hearing loss?"

"They must. Otherwise, I would have to believe no one told Gloria so that I would be blamed for holding up the bus. That's harder to believe than that they have selective hearing loss. Isn't it, Mrs. Kaplan?"

Mrs. Kaplan immediately dropped the subject of who held up the bus. She sighed mightily before resuming her smile. "Why, Margaret? Why do you reject all of our efforts to befriend you?" she asked as she reached out to cover my hand with hers.

I allowed her hand to rest on mine, looked her straight in the eye, and said, "Because you are destroying my self-image."

Even though the little chat did not end exactly there, that was where it hit bottom. That was when she popped up from the bed. And that is when the cookie crumbled. And that is when she sent me to Ms. Starr for the second time.

Jake remembered his mother's shock and dismay after that little chat. She had gone to her office to compose herself and to read over my file again, and then went to find him.

Earlier in the day, just about the time that Jake's mother was carrying cookies to Meadowlark, Cook had called Jake and asked him to come to the mess hall to fix her sink. The problem required nothing more than a plunger and took only a few minutes. When he finished, he saw the Sunday *New York Times* lying on Cook's cutting board. He asked Cook if she was done with it. She told him to help himself. So he did. He poured himself a cup of coffee and sat down with the newspaper. Coffee was not offered to the girls, and he helped himself only when they were gone—and not too often at that because he liked real cream in his coffee, and the best the mess hall had to offer was milk, and whether it was powdered or in the bottle, it was skim.

The mess hall was next door to the infirmary. Just as he sat down, he heard singing. *". . . Scatter her enemies / And make them fall, / Confound their politics . . ."* He looked out, and just above the lower edge of the window he saw a dark head moving toward the infirmary. Surprised that any of the girls were left in camp, he got up to see who it was. He recognized me, the Bartleby girl.

I was singing as I sauntered slowly toward my next encounter with Nurse Louise. He smiled to himself as he thought, She must have preferred not to go tubing on the lake. Keeping himself out of the window frame and in the shadows, he watched as I made my way to the infirmary. He heard, *". . . Frustrate their knavish tricks, / On Thee our hopes we fix, / God save us all!"* He watched until I was out of sight behind the infirmary door. As he sat back down with his coffee and his newspaper, he thought, How strange! No camper has ever sung that before.

He had hardly glanced at the headlines when his mother came into the mess hall, visibly upset. He saw that she needed to talk.

Mrs. Kaplan helped herself to a cup of coffee. Before she would allow herself to sit down, she said, "Jake, you will not believe what your Bartleby girl just said to us."

"Said to *us*? *Us*, Mother? This is Jake, remember. I am your son, your only son. Singular. You are my mother. My only mother. Singular. So who is *us*, Mother?"

Jake said he didn't know what had prompted him to

choose that moment to call his mother on saying *us* for *me* and *we* for *I*. After all, she had been doing it for years. Maybe it was timing: Having his Sunday morning interrupted first by Cook, now by her. Maybe it was just that there was something acid in this session's hot summer air. Maybe (and most probably), it was hearing "God Save the Queen" that did it.

Jake's remark caught his mother halfway between sitting and standing. She was undecided about whether she should get up and leave in a huff or sit down and have it out with her son. Jake made the decision for her. He took her hand. "Calm down, Mother. Just calm down. Let's talk about this. Tell me what Bartleby said."

Mrs. Kaplan sat.

She took a shallow sip of coffee and said, "When I asked her why she rejected all our efforts to befriend her, she said, 'Because you are destroying my self-image.'"

"What did you do?"

"I sent her to Louise."

"Nurse Starr?"

Mrs. Kaplan set her cup down. She nodded.

Jake evoked the image of me, that singular dark head poking its way to the infirmary, singing. As the sight came into focus, so did the song I sang. He hummed a little, and then, half to himself, he started to sing the first verse, the one he knew best, *"God save our gracious*

Queen,/Long live our noble Queen. ..." By the time he got to "*Happy and glorious,/Long to reign over us,*" he was singing out loud and when he got to the final line, "*God save the Queen,*" he was *con brio.*

Applying her smile like a cosmetic, his mother asked, "What did you just sing?"

"I was singing 'God Save the Queen.' Is my voice so bad that you don't recognize it? That Kane girl—Bartleby—was singing it just now." Full-voiced, Jake repeated, "*Happy and glorious,/Long to reign over us,/God save the Queen!*"

Mrs. Kaplan was too bothered to try to figure out why she was so bothered by that song. Instead she focused on the singer. "So," she hissed, "So," she repeated, "our Miss Kane, Miss Margaret *Rose* Kane was singing, was she? She was singing while I was agonizing over what she had just said?"

"Agonizing? I don't call sending her off to Louise Starr—"

His mother's head hurled back as if slung from a slingshot. The smile was GONE. What was happening? Her son had never spoken to her like this before. Never. *Who is us, Mother? ... I don't call ...* She stood up, stunned. She stayed in place seething, until she gathered breath enough to reply. "Well, Jacob, in the words of your protégée, I want this conversation to be over."

And she stormed out of the mess hall.

Jake watched her leave, shook his head sadly. He reopened the *New York Times*. He scanned the news—reading only the headlines and first paragraphs—and read the entire Arts section in depth before allowing himself to open the Sunday magazine and start the crossword puzzle. He had not yet taken his pen from his pocket when Ashley Schwartz found him. She smiled benevolently, and in a voice pitched as high as a dog whistle, she asked him if he enjoyed looking at the pictures. Jake gave her a loony smile and nodded.

Ashley told him that Gloria said that he should come with her. Jake did not get up immediately. He folded the paper and smoothed it down. She said that he'd better come now because one of the girls in Meadowlark had had an accident. In that same high-pitched voice she asked, "Remember the girl who wet her bed?" Jake returned a puzzled look. "The bed wetter?" she repeated. "She just threw up all over the floor in Meadowlark." And with that, she pantomimed retching. "THROW. UP. FLOOR. MEADOWLARK!"

He folded the paper again, studied it, smoothed it, hesitated. The temptation to set her straight was strong, but something told him that this was not the time. Ashley thought he hesitated because he didn't want to come or didn't understand the urgency. She scolded him, saying that it was starting to smell real bad. She waited for him to stand up. She pinched her nose and made a face. "Stinks. Stinky-poo. UNDER-STAND?" Jake nodded, slowly. "Gloria wants it cleaned up. NOW." She started to walk away, looked back, and saw that Jake still had not moved. Putting her hands on her hips, she asked if he understood NOW. Jake gave her one of his dopey smiles and started shuffling toward her. She turned her back to him and told him not to forget his bucket and mop and to remember which cabin. Meadowlark.

Jake took his time getting there, and once he did, he again stifled an impulse to *Frustate their knavish tricks.* Instead he silently went about the business of cleaning up the mess and never let the treasured alums know that he was on to them.

Now, as he watched the coffee dripping through the filter, he thought about the Meadowlarks, and he thought about me. The ratio had become Margaret Rose, one: Meadowlarks, seven, for he realized that Berkeley had become one of Them. He thought about all the mischief the Meadowlarks had put me through. They owed me, Bartleby.

He thought about the tactical error his mother had made in assigning the cabins. She too owed Bartleby.

And he thought about Alex and Morris and the towers. He owed them a backup plan.

And then, despite the gallons of coffee he had drunk all day, he fell asleep without unplugging the coffee-maker.

twenty-five

The following day, Jake was reluctant to leave his cabin. He knew that any news about our plan—good or bad—would come by phone. He quickly changed the lightbulbs in Hummingbird and came back to the cabin and waited for the phone to ring. He picked up the receiver to make sure there was a dial tone, then left to empty the trash cans into the Dumpster. Returned to the cabin, listened for a ring, checked again for a dial tone.

He was so jumpy that it was difficult for him to efficiently be his inefficient self.

He hurried through the rest of his chores, almost giddy with anxiety about his inability to conceive of a backup plan. It was Thursday, and he was due to haul the Dumpster down the hill for pickup, and he would have done so had there been some way to take the phone with him. But there was no telephone cord long enough to reach the bottom of the hill, so he risked his mother's wrath rather than risk missing a phone call. He left the trash in the Dumpster and hoped that it wouldn't attract rats or rabid raccoons or overflow before he could cart it away.

—everyone should always have a backup

Still worried and uneasy, Jake absentmindedly picked up his paintbrushes and began to dab paint on canvas. It was then that the idea came to him. It came to him all at once: What to do. How to do it. And why it would work. He was ready to run out of his cabin and put his plan in action when he remembered Uncle Alex saying that he got things done by not being in a hurry.

He would wait. Timing was all. He relaxed.

He tuned his radio to the classical music station, and as he applied paint to his canvas, he refined his plan and thought about the joys of payback time.

When my call came, he half expected the news to be bad—and it was—but it was bad in an unexpected way. The first time I told him that I was in jail, it didn't even register.

I'm in jail.

Who is this?

I'm who the operator said I am. I am Margaret Rose Kane.

Oh, that *Margaret Rose Kane.*

He needed time. He desperately needed time if he was not to hurry, and the timing of his backup plan was to work. He checked his watch. There were three business hours left to the afternoon. Peter Vanderwaal was on Central time, so he had an extra hour to make that call. He put his brushes aside, picked up the phone, and asked for directory assistance. He made three calls before phoning Peter. Then he and Peter talked at length because Peter always talked at length. When he hung up, Jake brewed a fresh pot of coffee.

And then he waited.

In the predawn darkness—well past lights-out and long before morning mess call—Jake stormed into Meadowlark cabin and snapped on all the overhead lights. He clapped his hands and shouted, "Up! Up! Everybody, up!" The girls were frightened, which is exactly what Jake had expected and of which he took full advantage. "Get dressed. Wear good tracking shoes, hats, and bring enough sunblock to cover yourselves from head to toe."

Ashley Schwartz was the first to speak up. "Who are you?" she asked.

Alicia asked, "You're not Jake, are you?"

"No, I'm his evil twin," Jake answered. "Now do as I tell you while I go get some supplies."

"Supplies for what?"

"For payback time."

"I'm going to Mrs. Kaplan," Ashley announced. "This is unauthorized, and I'm going to tell."

"I wouldn't do that just yet," Jake said. "I think we ought to have a little talk first." Defiantly, Ashley started toward the door. Without touching her, but with a stare as potent as a New Zealand Border collie, Jake herded her back to the row of girls, who were all standing now with their arms crossed over their chests, suddenly conscious of the fact that they were in their nightclothes in the presence of a grown man who was not an idiot. Keeping up his herding-master mode, Jake said, "Sit!" One by one, the girls sat. Three on the edge of one bed. Four on the one facing it. Jake stood in the aisle between the two. "Good!" he said after they had arranged themselves a wingspan apart. "Good!" he repeated. "Now we can talk."

He spun around and looked at each of the girls, passing by each one once. Then around again. "Let's begin with you," he said pointing directly to Berkeley Sims. "Yes," he said, "let's start with *Metalmouth* Berkeley Sims." There was a tittering wave that spread along one bed—the one on which Berkeley was seated—across the floor, and along the length of the other. Nothing Jake could have said or done would have better convinced them that this Jake knew more, saw more, heard more than they could ever have guessed.

"Where were you at camp last year, Miss Berkeley Sims?" he asked. Without waiting for an answer, he said, "Butterworth Cheerleading, wasn't it?" Berkeley nodded. "Is that where you learned the bed-wetting trick?" he asked. She nodded again. "I thought so. It's quite popular among cheerleaders. Let me see if I have this right. It goes like this: Two girls fill paper cups with urine—their own. They put them on the bathroom floor and leave. A third girl picks one up. Only one. The other is flushed down the toilet. Two others fill paper cups with water. One of the girls stands guard outside the door. Another climbs the ladder and stands on the top rung. First she spills the two glasses of water on the mattress to soak it thoroughly. She sprinkles the urine on top of that. The paper cups are thrown in the Dumpster by the kitchen trash. "So it takes . . . let me see"—here he pretended to count on his fingers— "oh, yes, it takes exactly seven to pull it off. If asked, you could say that none of you had peed in Margaret's bed, and technically, you would be correct."

The girls were speechless.

"Now, do I have it right?" he asked. They said nothing. "Tell me," he commanded, "is that the way you did it?" Like birds perched on a wire, they sat motionless. "Is that the way you did it?" he demanded. They nodded in unison. "I can probably tell who urinated in the cups and who climbed the ladder, but I won't. What is important is that I know who stood guard outside the door. That would be Berkeley. She did not participate other than standing guard and being the mastermind." He spoke directly to Berkeley. "I've seen it before, Berkeley. There are minor variations on the procedure, but in general, it is a trick that Butterworth Cheerleading excels at."

He folded his arms across his chest, studied the ceiling for a minute, then lowered his head. "Good," he said, summarizing. "Now that we have that little incident solved, who wants to talk about plumbing?"

The girls looked at each other and then sat back without saying a word, ready to listen to Jake's next tale. After all, this was all about them.

Again he addressed Berkeley. "Was that Pap Harris's Water-Skiing Camp you attended the year before last?" Berkeley nodded. "Did you forget to tell B-Cup over here," he said, looking straight at Kaitlin, "that she should never stuff into the drain the T-shirts of the girl you want to accuse? It's a dead giveaway that she did not do it. There's a better trick to stopping up shower drains, but I don't want to take the time now to educate you." He smiled. Then, looking at Stacey, he said, "And, Dolly, you really should not attempt to do dirty tricks until you know left from right. It might prove to be a problem a few years from now, when you learn to drive."

Then Kaitlin looked at Stacey. "We had all agreed it would be the shower on the left. Remember?"

Stacey was furious. "It depends on where you are. If you're inside the shower, it was the one on the right."

Kaitlin ranted, "Everyone else—everyone but you—understood that it was to be the shower on the left when you face them. Not when you're *in* them."

"Well now, enough of that," Jake said. "Do you want me to guess in whose cubby I will find the screwdriver that was used to loosen the drain plate?" He looked from one face to another until he saw Ashley smile. "Could it be Tattoo?" Ashley lifted her chin defiantly. "I know, I know, Ms. Ashley Schwartz, the screwdriver doesn't really belong to you. You lifted it. I know where it came from, and I know where it is stashed. Once you got rid of Margaret Rose, you weren't so worried about being caught with it. But I would like to get it back. As soon as we return from our mission will be fine."

He said nothing more for a while, allowing their uneasiness to grow. Jake waited until the pink of Ashley's blush deepened from petal to shocking. "Now," he said, "shall we talk about sun protection? Even though Berkeley tried hard to convince me that Margaret Rose had made the mess at the foot of her bed, I know she could not have. She was in the infirmary when Heather threw up. Besides, Heather—or should I call you *Fringie?*—from past experience, I know that at least one girl always comes back from tubing sick. So I hope your back is healed and that you have learned your lesson, for sunblock will be a very important part of your supplies."

He looked at each one of them. "Now, listen up. You'll need to use sunblock, so bring lots of it. And be sure to wear long sleeves. You are to be prepared for exposure to the elements. Remember, good shoes, long pants, sleeves, hats, and sunblock. I'll take care of the water supply."

Ashley popped up and said, "I still say that you can't do this. It's not an authorized activity."

"I'm going to see to that right now," Jake said.

Ashley said, "And I'm going to see Mrs. Kaplan and tell her that you are kidnapping us." She looked over at Berkeley and said, "You'd better come with me."

Berkeley said, "Skip it, Ashley. You heard him. We're going where he's taking us. Sit down."

Ashley tried one more time. "I'm going. Even if I have to go alone."

Jake said, "You are not going anywhere, Tattoo."

"Yes, I am."

"No, you aren't. Because I am. I'm going to see Tillie myself in a minute. Don't worry. She's going to authorize this activity. But first I'll tell you what you'll be doing and why you're going to be very grateful to me that I am giving you this opportunity to do it."

Kaitlin asked, "What reason could we possibly have to want to do anything you tell us to?" She folded her arms across her B-cups.

"Because you—all of you Meadowlarks—need to do something *for* Margaret Rose Kane instead of doing something *to* her. And you're going to thank me for giving you a chance to feel good about yourselves. I think Berkeley thanks me already."

The flush of embarrassment that had been fading from Berkeley's face started to deepen again, this time with the pink of pleasure.

Ashley sat down. Kaitlin calmed down. And they all listened attentively as Jake showed them pictures of the towers and told them his plan. "Get yourselves ready," he said, starting out the door. No one moved. He turned and saw the girls welded to their bunks. "Get dressed!" he commanded. "I'll be back with Tillie in half an hour. Remember, plenty of sunblock. But don't put it on yet. We have a long drive. I don't want any sunstroke or throwing up—before, after, or during."

As he closed the cabin door, he heard one of the girls

say, "Tillie? He called Mrs. Kaplan 'Tillie.' Twice. Who do you think he is?"

Berkeley said, "Her lover. All camp directors have one."

Mrs. Kaplan would not be persuaded until Jake told her that if she sanctioned his plan, made it official, she was far less likely to be sued by irate parents than if she did not. She could go along or she could resist, but either way, he was determined to follow through.

Mrs. Kaplan stared into the middle distance and pursed her lips. She played a game of Truth or Consequences with herself. If she agreed to make the trip "official," she would be given the chance to oversee the preparations and ensure the safety of the girls, as well as her good reputation. "For the sake of the girls, and as a community service, I'll do it."

"And with all due respect, Mother, in some small way this will compensate Margaret Rose for her having had such a miserable experience at Camp Talequa."

"Why did you choose that word—*miserable*?"

Jake shrugged. "Seemed accurate."

It was on the bus ride between Talequa and Epiphany that Berkeley Sims left her seat, walked to the front of the bus, picked up the microphone that was used for announcements, and began to sing.

"God save our gracious Queen,
Long live our noble Queen,
God save the Queen!"

She had not reached the end of the first verse
before everyone—everyone except Tillie Kaplan, but
including Jake, who was driving—joined in. By the
time they arrived at 19 Schuyler Place, everyone—
everyone except Tillie Kaplan—was in high spirits.

Phase One, Part B, and
Phases Two and Three

twenty-six

Even though I was back in my own genuine French provincial-style bed, I was once again convinced that I had not slept a wink until the sound of voices coming from outside awakened me. Before getting out of bed to investigate the voices, which in my half-awakened state I believed to be the men coming back, I studied the unfinished rose on the ceiling of my room. I wondered if Jake would finish it—or even try to—if the towers were no longer here to interest him.

I glanced at the clock. It was only six thirty. I guessed that the workmen wanted to get an early start since they had been unable to get any real work done the day before. I swung my legs over the edge of the bed and twisted my head from side to side to loosen the crick in my neck. The voices were quiet now, and I wondered whether or not I had really heard them, so I went to the window to look out.

And I saw the most remarkable sight.

Alicia Silver, Blair Patayani, Ashley Schwartz, Kaitlin Lorenzo, Stacey Mouganis, and Heather Featherstone filed out of the yellow camp bus and stopped by the back gate. Each of them spoke briefly to Jake and then followed his pointing hand to a place on one of the towers. Berkeley Sims was the last through the gate; she headed toward Tower Two, and only seconds later I saw her head and shoulders appear at my window. She saw me, too. She smiled and waved just before her head and shoulders disappeared from the window, and in quick succession her waist, stomach, legs, and feet appeared and just as quickly disappeared. She passed my platform and continued to climb, and finally she sat down on the narrowest rung, just below the clock faces and well above the roof of the house. I had to open the window, lean out, and twist my head to see her.

I turned away from the window to call my uncles but quickly turned back when I heard the squeal of the bus door. I could hardly believe my eyes. Climbing down the steps of the bus was no less a person than Herself, Mrs. Tillie Kaplan, owner and director of Camp Talequa.

She reached back into the bus and removed two six-packs of bottled water. Even from the distance of my bedroom window, I recognized the Evian label. Designer water! From Mrs. Kaplan.

Mrs. Kaplan said something to Jake that I could not hear. I saw Jake nod, listen, nod again, and then he pointed at me and waved. I jumped back and to the side, out of his line of sight, and called to my uncles. They were at my side in a heartbeat, took one quick look, and started down the steps with Tartufo hard on their heels.

The three of us made it to the edge of the service porch when we heard Jake roar, "STOP. DON'T TAKE ANOTHER STEP!"

We stopped on command.

Jake shouted, "Don't come here. The court has issued an injunction. You are not allowed in here. Don't risk it. If you try to stop the demolition now, you will be held in contempt of court. Don't tempt them into arresting you." He stopped, smiled directly at me, and added, "Again."

Mrs. Kaplan stepped forward. "We have a plan," she said.

Uncle Alex asked, "We?"

Mrs. Kaplan nodded, then swept her hand in the direction of the girls sitting in the towers. Three of them waved and greeted me with "Hi, Margaret."

Uncle Morris asked Mrs. Kaplan, "And who, may I ask, are you?"

"I am the director," she replied.

"Director? Of what?"

Any one of us could have answered that question,

but not one of us got a chance to, for we heard the back gate swing open as Tony came into the Tower Garden, and Tartufo, paying no attention to court orders, lunged at Tony, and Tony yelled at me, "Leash that animal."

I replied, "I'm not allowed to set foot in the yard. It's the law."

Jake said, "That's probably the piece of paper you have in your hand."

Tartufo came to Jake's side, stopped briefly, then, with his eyes and ears forward and his tail skyward, he took a stately walk toward the rear gate, where he lifted his leg and peed.

From their positions in Towers One, Two, and Three, the Meadowlarks laughed. Tony looked from tower to tower, shielding his eyes with his hand until he spotted Berkeley Sims perched high on Tower Two.

She waved.

He spun around and shook a fist at her. "You come down here this minute," he yelled.

Berkeley said, "I prefer not to."

Tony spun around again and waved his fist in all directions and hollered, "All of you. You cocky little she-brats. All of you, come down here this minute."

And in a chorus that was music to my ears, they said, "We prefer not to." And then they said it again. "We prefer not to." They said it again. And again.

And I understood that *we*. And I loved it.

The Meadowlarks perched in the towers caused hours of delay, and those cocky little she-brats stopped the demolition.

twenty-seven

Late on the previous afternoon, two local television stations and the *Epiphany Times* had gotten heads-up calls that there might be an interruption to the demolition of the towers at 19 Schuyler Place in Old Town. The newspaper assigned a reporter and a photographer to cover the story the next morning. The Channel 3's *Eyewitness News* team sent Holly Blackwell, their newest on-the-scene reporter who sensed a career opportunity.

On Friday as soon as a television van appeared in front of 19 Schuyler Place, so did a crowd. No one knew where the people came from, for ever since the Greater Comprehensive Redevelopment Plan had designated Schuyler Place as part of Old Town, the streets had been as quiet and dignified as the royal court of England. But television cameras find people or people find them. Either way, the street was jammed with young and old who wanted to wave at the camera. Others worked their way to the front of the line so that Holly could hold the microphone under their chins as they expressed their newly formed but deeply felt opinions of the towers and their fate.

When monitors at the Channel 5 studio showed that Channel 3's van was creating as well as capturing the breaking story, the program director of *FirstNews* sent a mobile unit and two reporters to the scene.

Jake made a hurried call to Peter Vanderwaal and suggested that he call Loretta Bevilaqua to find out if with her New York connections, she could parlay in-depth coverage from two local stations into coverage on at least one national all-news station. Peter called, and after twice reminding him that she, Loretta Bevilaqua, did not micromanage, she promised to see what she could do.

All day Friday, into the night, until the sun came up on Saturday, there were never fewer than six Meadowlarks up in the towers and never fewer than two cameras on them.

Mrs. Kaplan desperately wanted it over with. She wanted her campers back in camp. She needed them there. Sunday was parent-visiting day, and she was terrified that the Meadowlark parents would show up and their daughters would not. And neither would she.

Saturday, being a slow news day, the story of the sit-in at the towers got hot and hotter. The fact that not much was happening elsewhere plus the novelty of the situation in Epiphany—human interest, organized protest, local empowerment, outsider art—gave the national media enough to feed on. They came.

Peter Vanderwaal presented himself as an authority—which he certainly was—on outsider art, and he was interviewed by one of the national weekend anchors. He sat at the Uncles' old kitchen table and held up a sheaf of papers that he said were letters of support from art authorities, near and far. Never mind that, at that moment, all the letters had been written but only half of them had actually been signed. He waved the papers, flashed his smile and his diamond earring, and declared, "From Clarion State University right here in Epiphany, New York, to the Huntington Library, Art Collections, and Botanical Gardens in California, these towers are being called everything from a national treasure to a historical landmark. To call them masterpieces of outsider art would be an understatement."

Holly Blackwell wanted "in-depth coverage," as she called it, so she interviewed Mrs. Kaplan at length. She asked her what she regarded as her responsibilities toward the girls' safety versus her commitment to the towers. Mrs. Kaplan answered, "The safety of our Camp Talequa girls is always foremost in our minds. We consider this activity an urban Outward Bound-type learning experience. By halting the destruction of one of our nation's artistic treasures, this excursion is an experience in social responsibility as well. We teach both art and social responsibility at Camp Talequa. With the limited means we have at our disposal, we have dedicated ourselves to safeguarding these towers."

It was sweeps week for the towers.

By the end of Saturday suburban people who had never seen the towers, never even known of their existence, had an opinion about them.

DEFY AND OCCUPY was the next day's headline in the *Epiphany Times*. And because it was a slow news day, the paper published the entire text of Uncle Alex's appeal to the city council.

People magazine sent a photographer, who took pictures of the girls in the towers and told Mrs. Kaplan that the magazine would run the story the following week under the heading, OUTWARD AND UPWARD BOUND FOR ART. Mrs. Kaplan posed at the base of Tower Three, with two of the girls (Heather and Berkeley) visible. She smiled at the camera and for the cameraman. Jake's picture was not there at all. Neither was mine or the Uncles'.

CNBS, the national all-news cable channel, put Peter's interview on what they called a "loop," so that at least once every two hours, he got prime-time coverage. Of course, he was convincing. And adorable. In the week that followed, he got three marriage proposals and inquiries about job possibilities from fourteen recent art history graduates. He loved all the fame and fortune except for the marriage proposals. They depressed him.

Ever on the lookout for a way to outbroadcast the national broadcasters and to keep the story going, Holly Blackwell pursued City Hall for background on the story. Her many attempts to reach the mayor were unsuccessful. He was in South Carolina attending the National Mayoral Conference at the Hilton Head Golf and Country Club and was unavailable. His spokesperson said that the mayor would not have a statement until Monday, and, of course, there would be no demolition until he returned and had an opportunity to review both sides of the issue.

And that was time enough to stall.

And time enough for the Meadowlarks to get back to Talequa for visiting day.

And that was Phase Two.

twenty-eight

With Phases One and Two—STOP and STALL—completed, Loretta Bevilaqua saved the towers, just as she had promised she would.

Infinitel bought them.

—Whenever them big shots at Infinitel hear *Bevilaqua*, they know it means something
Loretta Bevilaqua knew that the next big thing in the telephone communications business would be wire-less—cellular—telephones. Cell phones are little radios that need towers to hold antennas to repeat signals from cell to cell, across a town or a state or from sea to shining sea.

Loretta Bevilaqua knew that giving the towers a useful purpose would not make them any more welcome in Old Town than they had been when they were useless. She also knew that for her purposes, the towers would function better if they were positioned at an elevation higher than downtown.

On Loretta Bevilaqua's recommendation, Infinitel

moved the towers to property that the company owned high on a hill above the university campus.

And them big shots knew that money could not buy the excellent free publicity Infinitel got from CNBS and *People* magazine.

twenty-nine

Uncle Morris drove me to the airport to meet my parents upon their return from Peru.

I had not seen them for a month, and I was excited. I had a lot to tell them.

That evening when I went downstairs to join them in the family room before dinner, I hoped to have them all to myself. But sitting on the sofa beside my father was a young woman who had been a graduate student of my mother's. I looked from my dad to that woman to my mother, and I knew that we would never again be the family we once had been.

I understood then why my parents had chosen to go to Peru without me. They needed time without me. Time to see if there was love enough between them— just them.

Beyond Phase Three

thirty

I never saw Mrs. Kaplan again, and except for Berkeley Sims, I never saw any of the Meadowlarks again either. Berkeley registered at Clarion State University the same semester I did. We saw each other occasionally—even had lunch together a couple of times—but no friendship ever grew out of it. After one semester, she dropped out of school to become a massage therapist. About a year ago, she sent me a copy of *People* magazine that featured her as the masseuse preferred by all the major male Hollywood stars. She had attached a Post-it to the page and written, *My second fifteen minutes of fame!* I saved the magazine.

—American woman in space
I have saved one other issue of *People* magazine. It is dated the same year as the one Berkeley sent me. I was glancing through it as I waited in line at the supermarket checkout. I bought the magazine along with my grapefruit juice and Boursin cheese when I saw it contained an article about a certain Anastasia Mouganis, who, as a

member of a volunteer group of NASA employees, answers queries sent in to NASA's Web site. The caption under the picture reads:

> Ms. Mouganis reports that the most frequently asked question is, "How do you go to the bathroom in space?" To this query, she replies with words and pictures using her vintage Cabbage Patch doll to demonstrate how astronauts must strap themselves into the WCS (waste collection system) to compensate for zero gravity.

And there was a picture of Anastasia—a.k.a. Stacey, a.k.a. Dolly—demonstrating that she had indeed learned left from right.

—El Niño . . . off the coast of Peru . . . caused disasters on almost every continent . . . at El Niño's peak . . . the angle of Earth shifted
Conditions off the coast of Peru caused the earth to shift but could not change the relationship between my parents.

—on the third Monday of January
My father moved out of our house. He married that young woman as soon as his divorce from my mother was final.

—Ma Bell broke up and gave birth to several independent low-cost long-distance communications companies
Infinitel set the towers in a parklike setting on top of the hill overlooking Clarion State University. They no longer zig and zag along the property line but are clustered together inside the iron pipe fence that was reshaped to encircle them.

—The Federal Communications Commission authorized . . . cellular phone services
Within four years of moving the towers, there were over one million cell phones in the United States, and the demand was growing.

Developers quickly saw the towers as a focal point for a new neighborhood. The main road leading up to the top was named Tower Hill Road. On either side of the hill, home builders were granted permits to carve out streets in a typical suburban pattern of curves and cul-de-sacs. One of those streets is called Clocktower Drive, and Alexander Place, a short street—only one block long—spans the distance between Morris Avenue and Rose Way. It is a nice neighborhood. Definitely upscale.

Gwendolyn and Geoffrey Klinger continue to keep their law offices at number 17 Schuyler Place, but seven years ago they started a family and moved. They bought a house on Alexander Place. Three of the young lawyers from Hapgood, Hapgood & Martin also moved to Tower Hill. So there they are, living in the neighborhood of the towers they had fought to destroy.

Like the Klingers, when my father and the woman he married started a family, they moved. They have a son named Connor, whom I happen to like a lot. They live at 184 Tower Hill Road in the very shadow of the towers that my father once called "useless" and "superfluous."

Infinitel appointed Jake as official conservator for the towers. He says that the job combines his best talents—janitor and artist. Jake visits Tower Hill at least once each season to do maintenance on the paint and the pendants.

Jake and Loretta Bevilaqua got married the summer after we saved the towers. I figure that he wanted to put to good use his experience at dealing with older, bossy women who have no sense of humor. There is the temptation to think of them as Mr. and Mrs. Bevilaqua because "for business she stays a Bevilaqua." Jake does his serious artwork at a studio in New York. I've never asked, but I'm sure Loretta pays the rent.

Last year there was a retrospective of the works of Jacob Kaplan at Peter Vanderwaal's museum in the Sheboygan Art Center. I flew to Wisconsin for the opening reception. Loretta took the time to attend. Even though I am as old now as Jake was then, the sutures holding the nip he took in my twelve-year-old heart loosened and wept when I saw him with her. I tried to like her. After all, she did save the towers; but she uses up all the air in the room, so I save my breath.

Peter has had his left ear pierced twice more, so with a three-hole punch, he has tripled his sparkle, and he is gaining weight, so with his added girth there is even more of him to be adorable.

The second summer after the towers were in place, the Uncles liquidated their inventory of "fun" watches and *occhiali antisole* and retired from the Time Zone. Uncle Alex continued to edit his roses, and Uncle Morris tended his peppers, but the two thirds of the backyard that had once been the Tower Garden was bare—planted with grass, nothing more. And where the iron pipe fence once stood there are hedgerows of privet to separate 19 Schuyler Place from its neighbors at 17 and 21.

My uncles lived long enough to see a new passion of rose roses climb and entwine itself along the fence. After they closed the Time Zone, Uncle Alex would take Tartufo to the top of Tower Hill for his evening walk. In the summer when the days were long and there was some remaining light after they had finished dinner, Uncle Morris would go with him. Their eccentricities—the Borsalino, the truffle hunting, the perpetual hand-waving arguments—were famous by then, and at dinner parties, people who lived on Tower Hill would tell each other of Rose Brothers–sightings. It became something of a contest to see who had the best story to tell. One resident of Clocktower Drive insisted that he had seen one of the Uncles jogging, wearing a warm-up suit. But everyone suspected that the teller of that tale was in need of a designated sighter.

When Tartufo died, by special permission of the city and of Infinitel, his ashes were scattered inside the fence at the base of the towers. He never found a truffle.

My uncles died within six weeks of each other. Alex, the younger, died first.

I inherited the house at 19 Schuyler Place. Like others who own these old houses, I converted the living room and dining room into offices and rewired the whole house for my computer consulting business. And like the Klingers, I remodeled the kitchen and added a room and a terrace in the back, but unlike them, I still live here.

I sleep in the small bedroom upstairs, the one with the "very distinguished, quite elegant," bedroom suite in genuine French provincial style. Its white is now as yellow as its gold-tone accents. But it is the rose rose ceiling that keeps me here. In a section in the far corner near the window that once looked out on the Tower Garden, there is a patch of a forgotten grid that is sketched but not painted. Jake has often offered to finish painting it, but I never let him.

The year after my uncles died, the city council commissioned a marker to be placed on the verge of the state highway just before the turn to Tower Hill Road. The marker explains that the towers were built by Alexander and Morris Rose and that they had been moved from their original location in Old Town. Even though the paragraph on the bronze marker is long and the lettering small, most people can read it, not because they are farsighted or rapid readers, but because most cars slow down as soon as the towers come into view.

From a distance, they strike the skyline like steel lace. Not until you get closer do they take on color—many colors—from orange sherbet to lemon and lime. No longer can anyone—except telephone linemen—stand under them and look up and farther up and watch the light hit the sheared blue surface of a shard of an old Noxzema jar or see a piece of amber Daum crystal dance in the light. The towers stand tall against the sky, silent symbols of a new neighborhood until a breeze comes from the direction of the old Glass houses, and then they sing a song of witness to the old.

So the history of the towers has not come to an end.

But the telling of it must.

Here.

Now.